He wanted to taste every delicious inch of her...

Jessica lay on the bed, her blouse half-open to reveal a peach lace bra that couldn't hide her erect nipples. The sight spurred Dan into action, and he ripped at his own shirt.

That got Jessica moving, too, and they raced to shed their clothes as if they were on fire. Which, in fact, they were. For each other...

By the time he got completely undressed, she'd reached the last stage—her panties. He held out a hand. "Stop."

Jessica obeyed, her gaze moving down his chest and his stomach, finally settling on his erection.

"Why am I stopping?" she asked, her eyes never moving up, not even an inch.

"I want to appreciate you just for a minute."

"Appreciate how?" She smiled.

"By looking," he murmured, climbing onto the big white bed. "And touching," he added, as his hands went to cup the most beautiful breasts he'd ever seen.

All Dan could think about was how stunning she was, and how lucky he was. How being inside her would be absolutely delicious. He wanted this to last forever. But time was running out....

Blaze™

Dear Reader,

Who says guys are the only ones who get to have *Arm Candy*? Not me, and not Jessica Howell, a woman who knows what she wants and isn't afraid to go after it. Unfortunately, she doesn't always know what she *needs*.

Take Daniel Crawford for example. Oh, Jessica wants him. To be her date, to be her lover. But to be her perfect match? To be the one man who makes her whole world make sense? She doesn't have a clue. Not until...

Anyway, Jessica is a lot like me when I was working my tail off in the movie industry. I had no room for anything but work, success and more success. Thankfully, I woke up and smelled the roses before it was too late, and so does Jess. But not until Daniel shows her a thing or two about what it means to love.

Affectionately yours,

Jo Leigh

Books by Jo Leigh

HARLEQUIN BLAZE

ARM CANDY

Jo Leigh

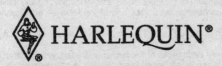

HARLEQUIN®

TORONTO • NEW YORK • LONDON
AMSTERDAM • PARIS • SYDNEY • HAMBURG
STOCKHOLM • ATHENS • TOKYO • MILAN • MADRID
PRAGUE • WARSAW • BUDAPEST • AUCKLAND

This book is for the dreamers—
all of us who can't live without books

ISBN 0-373-79126-7

ARM CANDY

This edition published by arrangement with Harlequin Books S.A.

Visit us at www.eHarlequin.com

Printed in U.S.A.

This guy is strolling on the beach in California. He sees a lamp, rubs it, and a genie pops out. The genie is so overjoyed that he decides to grant one wish to the guy.

The guy thinks about it and says, "I'd like you to build a highway to Hawaii because I'm afraid to fly." The genie tells him that it's impossible because of the depth of the ocean and the distance to Hawaii. So he asks the guy to wish for something else.

The guy thinks about it and, very enthusiastically, wishes he could understand women.

"Do you want the highway to have two or four lanes?" the genie says.

Source: Keidat, Ed; Keidat, Kim; Edelman, Joe "Genie in a Bottle"
http://www.coolquiz.com/humor/jokes/joke.asp?jokenum=3593

1

JESSICA WAS SECONDS away from a clean getaway. At a quarter to midnight on a Thursday night, she figured everyone else had left Geller and Patrick, Inc., and she could simply go to the elevator and make it to the street and a taxi without interference. Wrong. Wrong. Wrong.

Owen McCabe, her boss, her former mentor and current major pain in the butt, popped out of his office one second before she pressed the down button. Not only did he scare the bejesus out of her, but he also made her drop her portfolio, which gave him an excuse to rush over and help her pick up her papers.

"Burning the midnight oil, Jess?"

"Yep, and now I'm exhausted, so if you'll just give me the—"

"I know," he said, handing her the prospectus on the new eyeshadow line, "why don't we go get ourselves a nice nightcap. That'll help you get right to sleep."

She took a deep breath as she slipped the papers back into the portfolio. "Thanks, Owen, but I don't need any help. Just a taxi."

"I've got my car right downstairs."

"No, that's okay. You go on home. I'm sure Ellen's worried that it's so late."

"She went to bed hours ago," he said. "The boys had track today and they wore her out."

"I understand how she feels." Jessica pressed the down button again and silently prayed for the elevator to arrive.

"So," Owen said, leaning against the wall in a not-so-casual effort to appear relaxed, "you all set for next week?"

"Pretty much. Just a few more odds and ends. We'll be fine. It's going to be a huge success."

"Yeah, yeah, it will. Mostly due to your efforts."

"Nonsense. Everyone's been working like dogs."

"With you as captain and commander."

Six months ago she would have been thrilled by the compliment, but things had changed.

Somewhere along the way, her boss had gotten the idea that the two of them could be more than co-workers. Despite the fact that he was married with twin boys. Despite the fact that she'd never given him a smidgen of encouragement. Despite the fact that he knew she had no time or desire to date anyone, period.

She'd given the situation a lot of thought. She could complain about harassment, make a stink, but for all practical purposes, she'd ultimately be the loser. No matter the outcome, a suit would put a very large dent in her career plans. Instead, she'd decided to deal somehow with Owen until the new line was in place, then, with that success under her belt, make her move. Revlon had expressed interest in her, and she was pretty sure there was going to be a shake-up at Clinique. All she had to do was get through the next two weeks without a major fiasco, and she could write her own ticket.

"Sure I can't persuade you?" Owen asked as the elevator doors hissed open.

"Not tonight. Thanks anyway, I appreciate it."

He touched her arm as she walked into the car. "And I appreciate you."

She smiled until the doors closed, then she let out a loud groan. God, what a nightmare. And it was only going to get worse.

In four days, the new line would be launched with one of the most elaborate campaigns and media focus in cosmetics history. A solid week of high-impact promos featuring A-list celebrities, all taking place in Manhattan with locations from the Rainbow Room to Central Park, and she was in charge of seeing that nothing went wrong. Luckily, her team was top-notch, especially her assistant, Marla, which meant she could concentrate on putting out fires rather than concerning herself with the details. Unfortunately, the biggest fire she'd have to put out was in Owen's pants.

To make matters worse, they were all staying at the Willows hotel for the duration, and Owen had booked her a suite right next to his own. Undoubtedly with connecting doors.

Something had to be done. Something that wouldn't get her fired. Something that would show Owen once and for all that she wasn't available.

The elevator stopped in the lobby and she nodded at the security guy as she headed for the street, her heels clicking on the marble floors. Once she was outside, she stood still for just a moment, letting the cool air of the early-fall evening refresh her. This was her favorite time of year, especially in New York. The whole city seemed more alive. The humidity and heat of summer had finally passed, and the promise of brilliant holidays shimmered just around the corner.

She stepped to the curb and hailed a taxi. In another ten minutes or so, she could take a nice warm shower, crawl between her Egyptian-cotton sheets and forget about Owen, makeup and ad campaigns until five-thirty, when it would all begin again.

The cabbie was mercifully silent, and Jessica leaned her head back on the torn seat. There was so much to do before the premiere, and she felt guilty about leaving work at all.

Ridiculous, but nonetheless it was true. Her job was everything... No, that wasn't true. Her *career* was everything. Nothing, not even Owen and his out-of-control libido, was going to stand in her way. She would be an executive VP before she reached thirty, or die trying.

But that meant fending off Owen's advances until the campaign was over. The only thing that would keep Owen away was her having a boyfriend. But he knew she didn't have one, and how in hell was she supposed to come up with one in the next week?

Her gaze flickered over the staccato images flashing by the window as the taxi zoomed toward Chelsea. At the corner of Seventh Avenue and West Twenty-first, she saw a billboard for Angel's Escort Service.

Jessica smiled as she stared, the entire plan falling into place with a sweet little *plunk*. An escort. Of course. She could say it was someone from Harvard, someone she'd been with before. It would be a simple enough thing to hire a man for the job, someone sophisticated enough to play the part, handsome enough to look good in the inevitable photos, and someone discreet enough not to blow the whistle on her.

Glen. Her best friend. Of course. God, why hadn't she thought of this before? It was so obvious. The only person in the whole office who'd even heard of Glen was Marla, and Marla was the soul of discretion. She'd call him tomorrow. He'd love a week at the Willows. And Owen McCabe could take his advances and shove them right up his Armani.

"LOVE TO. Can't."

Jessica blinked, not wanting to believe the words. "Glen, no. Please. Maybe you don't understand the seriousness of the situation. He's relentless. He's everywhere. I need you."

"I know, Jess, but I just can't, I'm sorry."

"Why?"

"Well, for one thing, I'll be in California for four of the days."

"You can't cancel? Reschedule?"

His deep baritone filled her ear and made her clutch the phone with a desperate fist. "No, I can't."

"Dammit, dammit, dammit. This was the perfect solution."

"So, find someone else. Surely I'm not the only guy you know."

"No, but you're the only guy I know well enough to ask. Come on, Glen. You're perfect."

"Ah, you say the sweetest things."

"How about a friend? You have friends. Lots of friends. I'll pay. Well. But he's got to be discreet. If anyone finds out…"

"I think I might know someone."

"Really?" She grabbed her Mont Blanc, the pen she'd gotten as a graduation present from her aunt Lydia of Belgium, and twirled it between her fingers.

"Yeah, but I'll have to convince him."

"Do it. Please. I'm begging."

"Hey, I'll do my best."

She could picture him sitting in his gallery, underneath the Jean-Michel Basquiat collage, wearing something fabulous that flattered his blue eyes and dark, dark hair. "Thank you."

"Just a thought," he said, "but have you tried telling your boss you're not interested?"

She laughed, which she hadn't done in quite some time. It wasn't a good laugh, though, and she thought of the many, many times she'd told Owen straight out that she had no intention of stepping over the line with him. "He has selective hearing. And don't tell me to file a suit. I've thought this through and I'm going to bail when the time is right.''

"I figured. You're nothing if not thorough."

"You make it sound like that's a bad thing."

"Make that thorough and paranoid."

She smiled. "When this is all over, I'm going to buy you the most decadent meal in Manhattan. You say where and when."

"Deal. Now let me go see what I can do."

"Go!" She hung up, then leaned back in her chair, consciously relaxing her shoulders as she sank into the kidskin leather. Glen would come through, she had to believe that. If not, she'd just plain hire someone from an escort agency. She'd heard of it being done, although she'd never met anyone who'd used the service. But she hoped she didn't have to resort to that. This was too important.

A knock on the door brought her back to the business at hand. "Come in."

Marla Scott, Jessica's assistant, walked in, her arms filled with magazines. She came over to the desk, put them down carefully, then rubbed her hands together. "I've marked all the ads. Check out *The New Yorker*. There's a column raving about the budget and our conspicuous consumption. It's great."

The stack was huge, and this was only the beginning of the blitz that would blanket newspapers, radio and billboards across the city. By the end of the campaign there wouldn't be a man, woman or child in the country who wouldn't know about the New Dawn line.

Marla sat down in the chair across from Jessica. "So are you up to your elbows?"

"Yes, but talk anyway."

"Okay," she said, flicking a strand of her long red hair away from her face. "So I went out with this John person last night. The one from the Starbucks? Who got the last oat scone?"

Jessica remembered. Poor Marla. Shy as a butterfly, and so lonely. She was the best assistant Jessica had ever had, completely on top of the job, no nonsense, but also generous and funny, and she had the absolute worst luck with men. "He's the tall one, right? NYU?"

Marla nodded. "Lookswise, scrumptious. Datewise, disastrous."

"No."

"Yes. He took me to a play. Off-off-Broadway. More like performance art, really, with this one woman complaining about her period while this other woman pretended to masturbate. It was very high on the yuck factor."

"It wasn't his fault it was terrible."

"True. Very true."

"So?"

"So it turns out the woman pretending is actually his ex-girlfriend, only by the time we're backstage schmoozing with the cast and fans, they're not so ex, if you know what I mean."

"What?"

"Complete with kissage. I mean, they moved behind a poster of *The Vagina Monologues*, but I could still see them all over each other."

"Oh, God."

"He didn't even pay for the taxi home."

"Bastard. He deserves someone who pretends to masturbate onstage."

"My sentiments exactly. Only..." She looked down at her lap, to the hunter-green skirt she loved so much. "...he made me laugh at dinner. And I was so...I don't know."

"Yeah."

Marla smiled purposefully. Adamantly. "No big. I'll just keep, you know, trying. Never give up. That's my motto.

Not till you're old and toothless and have all the cats that can fill an apartment.''

"I'm sure it won't come to that."

"Probably not. But it's good that I'm not allergic. To cats, I mean."

Jessica shook her head, and wished she had something akin to a social life where she might be able to meet someone right for Marla. But since her entire entourage consisted of Glen, who was gay, her mother, who lived in Cincinnati, and her landlord, who made an art out of complaining while not actually doing anything, there didn't seem to be much hope.

"If there's not anything else," Marla said, "I'm going to call the Zephyr agency and double-check on the models."

"No, that's good. Thanks."

Marla stood up, and headed for the door. But before she went out, she turned back. "Do you think we have a chance of getting Shawn?"

Jessica leaned back in her chair. "Who knows. We're certainly offering him enough money."

"Can you imagine? Shawn Foote in the same room? I'd get all swoony, I just know it."

"He may be hunky, but he's just a guy."

Marla leaned her head to the right and quirked her lips. "Just a guy? I think not. He's…he's…"

"The Uberhunk. I know."

Marla nodded. "I'll report back."

Jessica looked down at the spreadsheet on her desk and forgot all about male models, dating fiascos and even her own personal problems. Seconds later, the world outside her office could have crumbled and she wouldn't have noticed.

DAN CRAWFORD WAS at sixes and sevens. Which was an interesting expression he'd just looked up on his computer.

Seems it came from an old French game called Hazard, and had something to do with difficulty in shooting dice. But knowing what the term meant didn't help the situation. He had to make a decision, and neither of the two immediate options appealed all that much.

Okay, so he could take the job in Botswana. He liked Africa, and hadn't been there for almost fifteen years. It would be a challenge, and the company, an international trading firm, had been after his consulting services for a long time. But it would mean a commitment of almost a year, which seemed excessive.

On the other hand, he could partner up with Zeke on the Baja 1000 race, but that would mean a whole hell of a lot of training, getting the car up to specs, moving down to L.A. until the race, and, of course, being with Zeke, who was a great guy unless he got too drunk, which he did whenever he raced.

Dan's gaze moved next to the fireplace, to the glass cabinet where he kept his mementos. The large second-place trophy from the Baja three years ago taunted him. Then he looked at the bookcase, at the pile of papers and articles he'd collected, everything from the psychology of racing to the topography of Baja. Damn, he'd put in a lot of man-hours on winning. So why wasn't he more interested? Zeke wasn't *that* bad. And if Dan supplied the booze, he could maybe rig it so his buddy couldn't get so much of it.

He got up from his desk and walked over to the window. From the fifteenth floor he could see the bookstore on the corner, Villard's Books, big, independent and as quirky as his own tastes. The staff there indulged him and his projects, the more obscure the better. In fact, between the New York Public Library, Villard's and the Internet, he could research anything to his heart's content.

Maybe he'd go down now, browse through the travel

section, have a cup of coffee. Come up with something new to discover, or as his mother would say, bury himself in a new obsession.

He headed for the bedroom, but before he made it there, he got buzzed from the lobby. Crossing to the door, he answered the intercom. "Yeah, Jimmy?"

"Someone to see you, Mr. Crawford. Glen, uh, what's that?"

Dan heard a mumble in the background. Then, "Glen Viders."

"Great, send him up." Dan let go of the buzzer, curious. He'd known Glen for about a year, mostly as someone who kicked his ass regularly at racquetball. He liked Glen, liked his sense of humor and his taste in art. He'd bought a Lichtenstein from his gallery and he'd paid a good price for it. But they'd never really socialized, except for the occasional showing invitation. What could bring him by?

Dan opened the door and invited Glen in.

"This isn't a bad time, is it?"

"Not at all. I was just going to make some coffee. Would you like some?"

"Sure."

Dan led the way into the kitchen, where he pulled the beans out of the fridge to begin the process. "So, what's up?"

"I have a proposition for you."

Dan stopped short. "Oh?"

Glen laughed. "Not that kind of proposition. This one should be more to your liking."

Smiling, and a touch relieved, Dan continued with the coffee making. "Intriguing. Do go on."

Glen leaned against the kitchen door, crossed his arms over his chest and smiled. "I have this friend. Her name is Jessica Howell and she's got a problem."

Dan worked on the coffee while Glen filled him in on

the situation. His first instinct was to say no and be done with it, but the more he heard about Jessica, the more an idea began to germinate. "So she's brilliant, huh?"

"Top two percent of her class at Harvard. She's razor-sharp, and too damn articulate for that foolish job she's got."

"Workaholic?"

"Beyond belief. I don't think she's been on a date since she moved to New York six years ago."

"And I'd be with her. In her room for the whole week?"

"Yeah. Well, wait. I'm not sure about the 'in her room' part. But you'd have to stick pretty damn close."

"Hmm."

"Who knows? Things could go that way, if you play your cards right."

"And what did you say she looked like?"

Glen smiled. "I didn't. But now that you ask, she's a babe. A little thing, but a powerhouse, if you know what I mean. Auburn hair, blue eyes. Really striking. She could have the men lining up, but—"

Dan nodded, pleased, but not all that concerned. Her looks were incidental. Her mind was what interested him. She was willing to pay to have an escort. He didn't need the money, but he did have something he wanted to bargain for. "Tell you what. Set up a meeting. Whenever it's convenient for her. We'll talk."

"She'll be thrilled."

"Maybe. Maybe not."

Glen pushed himself off the wall. "What are you plotting?"

"Quid pro quo, Glen. With some very exciting potential."

Women...

If you praise her, she thinks you're lying
If you don't, you're good for nothing
If you talk, she wants you to listen
If you listen, she wants you to talk
If you visit her often, she thinks you're boring
If you don't, she thinks you're cheating
If you're jealous, she says it's bad
If you're not, she thinks you don't love her
If you stare at other women, she accuses you of flirting
If other men stare at her, she's flattered
If you want sex, she says you don't respect her
If you don't, she thinks you're gay.

Source: Thomas, Megan ''Men are Marvelous Creatures.''
http://www.cs.berkeley.edu/~mct/funny/woandmen.html

2

GLEN STARED AT HIM for a long moment, clearly trying to figure out whether or not he would move forward. "I'll call her tonight," Dan finally said with a slow grin.

"Great."

The coffee aroma filled the kitchen, and Dan got down two mugs. "Can I ask how come you're not the one who's stepping up to the plate?"

"Hey, I'd do it in a minute, but I have to be in L.A. Besides, I think this will work out better."

"Oh?" He got out the cream from the fridge, took it and the mugs to the butcher-block table. He nodded for Glen to take a seat, and made a pass at his pantry. He brought out a couple of boxes of cookies. By then the coffee was ready, so he carried the pot over and poured.

"Jessica and I go back to college, and I'd say I know her pretty well. Inside that ambition is one hell of a good woman. She just has to take off the blinders. See something of the world around her. From what I've heard, that seems to be your specialty."

Dan sat down. "Curious perspective, and I suppose reasonably accurate."

"Yeah. You two will be…interesting."

"I wonder why she hasn't just put the kibosh on the boss. Doesn't he know there are laws?"

"According to Jessica, she doesn't want the hassle. She's planning a move upward after her campaign is a raging success."

"Got it. Always looking at the next step, eh?"

"Never misses the details on a spreadsheet."

"But almost gets hit by the bus?"

Glen grinned, and lifted his coffee mug. "To new adventures."

Dan clicked his mug but, instead of taking a sip, he said, "Hey, why don't you give Jessica a call now? See if she can meet me for a drink tonight."

Glen pulled out his cell phone and dialed. By the time he hung up, the arrangements were made, and Dan had two hours to put together his counterproposal.

If it worked, it was going to be one hell of a lot more exciting than any race.

JESSICA CHECKED OUT her appearance in the window of the bistro. The weather had been kind to her hair, she'd reapplied lipstick in the cab, and her Donna Karan suit looked as if she'd put it on a half hour ago. Not that it mattered. She was the one doing the hiring, but still. The situation was just awkward enough to have a built-in nervousness factor of ten, minimum.

Dan Crawford. She'd done an Internet search on him, and what she'd seen had taken her utterly by surprise. The man was a very highly paid computer consultant and had worked for some of the biggest financial institutions in the world. His prices must be astronomical, causing her to call Glen back and make sure he hadn't promised she'd pay the man her entire yearly wage. Glen had assured her that if Dan Crawford did this, it wasn't going to be for the money. Which begged the question…

Why? Why would he give her odd little proposal a moment's thought? What could he possibly get out of it, if not money?

She was about to find out. If she could get her legs working and walk inside. After a deep breath and a little pep talk, she yanked on the hem of her jacket, pushed her hand-bag strap up on her shoulder and walked inside.

Dorian's was an upscale Wall Street bar. Martinis of all flavors dotted the tall tables in the bar, hoisted by the young and the restless go-getters in their Prada and Emporio Armani. Not much laughter, but a lot of chatter, caromed off walls decorated with three-dimensional art, mostly in shiny metals or rusted copper. It worked, especially with the oak bar and tables.

She walked a little farther, until she was midway between the door and the bar itself, then did a quick perusal. No one looked like Dan Crawford, although one young man to her right bore a marked resemblance to Colin Firth. She kept scouting.

Her reward came seconds later. At the far right edge of the bar, a man, alone, saving a seat, looked up expectantly. He was pretty damn close to Glen's description. Around thirty-five. She couldn't tell if he was six foot three, but he had that tall, lanky look about him. Dark hair, smooth, shiny, thick, parted on the right. Wide eyes, generous mouth, and a nose just a wee bit big for his face. Altogether a striking combination. A little too striking.

Glen hadn't said anything about him being gorgeous. The word hadn't come into play once. And she knew from experience that Glen knew gorgeous. So maybe it wasn't Dan.

The man in question waved, quashing her doubts. He stood. Yep. Six-three at least. Smiling, too. A great smile. A smile that multiplied the gorgeous by a factor of six.

She pasted her own smile on her face and made her way through the crowd. He manfully held on to the two bar stools, chasing away a blonde with boobs the size of grape-fruits.

"I really hope you're Jessica Howell," he said as soon as she was in earshot.

"I am."

"Good because this is the only empty seat in the place. Guess I should have suggested somewhere quieter."

"There isn't anyplace quieter. Not around here at least."

He held out his hand. Long, supple fingers, strong grip. Warm, but not at all damp. She felt her cheeks heat just from the touch, which wasn't like her. Not at all.

"Sit. Let me buy you a drink."

"I should be the one buying."

"Next round, if you want," he said. "What's your pleasure?"

"A Merlot, please."

He nodded, then turned to get the attention of the bartender as Jessica climbed up on the stool. Being so short, it was always an iffy proposition, but she didn't flash anyone on her way up. She put her handbag on her lap and glanced at Dan. He was even better-looking close up. It was his lips, of course. Pouty, full, but incredibly masculine. Laugh lines etched on each side. If Marla were here, she'd wax rhapsodic about their kissability. Their smoochiness. Ah, that Marla. She had a way with words.

Dan put his credit card on the bar when the drinks arrived. He'd ordered a German lager, and he didn't bother pouring it into the iced stein. Instead, he took a long pull from the bottle, giving her an enticing view of his Adam's apple.

Her gaze moved down to his shirt. White oxford, well tailored, silk, she'd bet. It fit him beautifully, and she liked that he'd rolled up the sleeves a couple of turns. His jeans surprised her, but then she realized he wasn't tied to a company, and he could wear any damn thing he liked. The jeans got her vote. They were good old-fashioned Levi's and they fit his tall, yummy body like a glove.

He coughed, and she almost spilled her wine in an attempt to get her gaze up and away from where it'd been focused. Again with the blushing. Good God, what was the matter with her? She must be getting her period. She was never this…aware.

"Glen filled me in on your dilemma."

"So he said, but I want to make sure you understand completely before we go any further."

"Absolutely."

"It's really an acting job. I assumed he'd know someone out of work who could use the money. I can't imagine why you'd be at all interested."

"I'll tell you. But first, let me hear what you expect."

She sipped some wine, felt it melt all the way down, easing a bit of her nervousness. "I've got a boss who's completely out of control, and I need someone to pretend to be my lover for the week. We're launching a line of cosmetics with a huge press bash and back-to-back junkets. Whoever I hire is going to have to be available for any or all of the events. For meals. For anything, all the while acting like we're the couple of the decade."

"Yep, that's pretty much what Glen said."

"Okay, so why would you be interested? I have to tell you, I almost didn't come. He twisted my arm, made me promise to see you. But I don't get it."

"Well, Jessica, I think there's something we could do for each other. I see your problem, and while I'm not an actor, I think I could play the part. I'm a quick study, and I have no social ties that would interfere."

"But?"

He smiled with those lips of his. She almost giggled like a coquette.

"Here's what I want," he said, studying her eyes. "I want access."

"Access?"

He nodded. "To you."

"Pardon me?"

"To your thoughts."

She opened her mouth, but the only thing that came out was a kind of cluck.

"All of them."

"What the hell are you talking about?"

He laughed. The sound was rich and deep and almost enough to make her stop questioning his sanity. Almost.

"Okay, let me explain."

"Please do."

"I'm a curiosity junkie. Can't help it. It's a long, long story, full of interesting tidbits about my eccentric upbringing and my parents' radical philosophy, which I'm sure we'll discuss in detail over the next week, but the upshot is, I live to get answers to the big questions. I studied physics with some of the greatest minds on the planet, and theology in Rome and Israel. I've challenged my senses, my abilities, and always attacked the major problems of my life head-on. I might quake in my boots, but I do it until I'm satisfied. Which doesn't mean I'm always successful. But I never wonder what would have happened if only I'd dared."

"And what has that got to do with pretending to be my boyfriend?"

He laughed again. "Everything. Because what I want from you is answers."

"To what questions?"

"All of them."

"Excuse me?"

"All of them about women."

"I don't know all the answers about women."

"But you know the answers for you."

She gave him a long look.

He grinned back at her. "No, I'm not certifiable. Nuts, yes. But not quite at the padded-room stage."

"You want answers about women?"

He nodded.

"What does that mean?"

"It means, I get to ask you anything. No holding back. No thinking twice about propriety. I ask, you answer. Honestly. To the best of your ability. All the questions I've wanted to ask but haven't dared."

"You've never dated?"

"Oh, I've dated. Many times. I've had relationships. All of which have failed. Mostly, I fear, due to my fumbling. My lack of understanding. Seriously, I don't get it. Screw physics and the Big Bang theory, the great imponderable isn't God, it's women. Who are you people? The books are useless. Believe me, I've read them. Everything from *Men are from Mars* to Dr. Phil. And I still don't get you.

"Every time I think I've figured you out, I'm totally thrown for a loop. Take Tamara. Great gal, an incredible dancer. I was crazy about her, and she swore she loved me. We lived together for two blissful years. So what happened? Right after I proposed, and we're talking days here, she moved in with a drug addict who beat her for a hobby. And she's just the tip of the iceberg. I ask other men, and they either throw up their hands or give me advice that lands me in the doghouse. It's nuts, and it's crazy, and dammit, what I want is to once and for all get it."

Jessica heard what he said. She was a little taken aback by his earnestness and enthusiasm, and completely certain this wasn't going to work at all.

"Oh, no," he said. "Don't make up your mind yet. Please."

"I just don't think—"

"Look, I know it sounds crazy, but really, it's not. It's like a research project. An in-depth study. Think of me as an anthropologist. It won't be scary, I promise. And I won't use the information to hurt you or anyone else. But come on. This is a once-in-a-lifetime opportunity. I'd never get this kind of access. In real life, I'd be too afraid to ruin a relationship. Or if I paid for it, I'd never really be sure I was getting the real juice, you know? But this way, when we both can win, and there's no feelings to hurt or wound, then, well…"

"Not to be immodest, but I think I can convince your boss or anyone else that I'm your man. I won't embarrass you. I know my way around the press, and I won't cost you a penny. All you have to do is answer me honestly. If you don't know the answers, great. No sweat. But if you do know, then I want them. No political correctness. No shading or hedging. Just what's what."

"What's what, huh? Well, I know one thing."

"Go on."

"I need a much stronger drink."

Dan held his grin steady, and made sure not to look too satisfied. She was gonna go for it. A minute ago he'd thought all was lost, but now? She was intrigued. From what Glen had told him about her, he'd hoped she'd be curious. "What kind of stronger drink?"

"A whiskey sour, please. Make it a double."

"Good choice." He signaled the bartender again, and while he waited his turn he took his time looking her over. He'd been so busy studying her body language that he hadn't properly appreciated her body.

She was little, but not girlish. In fact, if he'd had to describe her, the word that would fit the bill was *vamp*. Sort of a throwback to an older age, Rita Hayworth, say, or Veronica Lake. The red hair had something to do with it, maybe the soft way it curled on her neck, or the swoop over her right eyebrow. Her lips, too, seemed naturally full, not collagen-injected like so many of the tonier crowd. And if they had been helped? Who cares. She was lush and her skin seemed silky, and the intelligence so clear in those blue eyes made him want to start his week tonight.

Not that he was going to actively pursue more than his stated objective.

"What'll it be?"

He started at the bartender's voice, ordered her drink, and himself a single-malt scotch, neat. When he turned back to Jessica, she pushed her hair back behind her left ear. Her hand, neat, tiny, feminine, captured his gaze and held it. He watched as she put her fingers around her wineglass. Rubbed the rim lightly.

Okay, so maybe he would pursue something more. Hadn't Glen said she'd been solo for quite some time? Hadn't he himself been entirely too celibate for longer than was healthy?

"Dan?"

"Yes?"

"What are you going to do with this information, assuming you get it?"

"Use it."

"For a book? A degree?"

He shook his head. "I hadn't thought of that, but I wouldn't rule out the idea. Actually, I'm doing this for my own personal edification."

"Meaning you're looking for a wife?"

"Wife, lover, significant other. Yeah."

"I'd think women would be banging down your door."

"Not the problem. Quality is the issue. I'm looking for what my parents had. Which, in my naiveté as a young man, I figured all parents had."

"A good relationship?"

"Much more than that. My folks were, and you'll pardon the cliché, two halves of the same whole. They were married thirty-nine years, and were more crazy about each other when my father died than the day they met. That's what I want. A partner. A best friend. All of it."

"Tall order."

"Don't I know it. Hence, the quest."

She gave him a half smile. "I've never been part of anybody's quest before."

The drinks arrived right then, and Dan handed the whiskey to Jessica. "So you'll do it?"

She took the glass, sipped, closed her eyes, opened them again. "I'll do it."

He toasted her, the clink ringing clearly against all the muddled noise around them. "Fantastic." He brought his own drink to his lips, then hesitated. "So when do we begin?"

"Monday."

"The Willows?"

She nodded.

"Great. I'll check in that afternoon."

Jessica's eyes widened. "Whoa, cowboy. Check in?"

He downed his scotch, ready for this. "Well, sure."

"No, no, no. You're not staying there. Just appearing when needed."

He gave Jessica his most innocent, sincere smile. "That would be a royal pain in the ass for both of us. Much simpler to be there. But don't worry. You have nothing to fear. I know the suites there and I'll sleep on the couch."

She gave him an "I don't know" look.

"Check with Glen. He'll tell you I'm harmless. Besides, I don't want anything getting in the way of the research. And sleeping together would really screw things up."

Her eyes softened. The internal debate went on a few more seconds, then she sighed. "It would keep Owen off my back."

He nodded. "This is gonna be great."

"That is highly unlikely. I'll be happy if it's survivable."

"Come on. You'll knock 'em dead."

Jessica shook her head, causing her hair to shimmer in the lights. He hadn't lied when he'd said sleeping with her would screw things up. But maybe he could ask all his questions real fast.

*Five things you'll NEVER hear one
guy say to another guy:*

1. *Does my butt look fat in this?*

2. *I'm tired of beer.*

3. *Yours is bigger than mine.*

4. *You know what always makes me cry? Those long-distance commercials.*

5. *Our team lost 10–1. But we tried our best, and after all, that's the important thing.*

Source: Thompson, Dave ''Things You'll Never Hear''
http://www.ijmc.com/archives/

3

"DANIEL, HONEY, I love you, but isn't this just a bit nutso, even for you?"

Dan smiled up at his mother. "Probably. But then, it's your fault."

Colleen Crawford put down her mug of coffee and gave him a look. "And how did you arrive at that conclusion?"

"If you'd just talk to me, I wouldn't have to hire myself out to strange women."

"We're talking right now."

"But not about what I want to know."

She took another sip and leaned back in her beat-up old director's chair. They were on her balcony, looking out over her garden, the pride and joy of her life. Aside from him, of course. She grew all her own vegetables, flowers, anything she took a fancy to. For the most stubborn, there was a small greenhouse. The rest just gave in and grew, somehow knowing his mother wouldn't let up until they sprouted. HGTV had done a profile on her green thumb. Of course, it hadn't hurt that she was so well-known for her books, but still. The show had been about the garden.

"We've discussed this," she said. "Some things have to be discovered. Not taught."

"Even when I've got the inside track on one of the world's leading experts right here?"

"There are no experts on relationships, pumpkin. Only wild-ass guesses."

"I suppose that's what you teach at NYU?"

''Precisely.''

''So if there are no answers, what's the use of searching?''

''Because the only answer *is* the search.''

''Right.''

''You'll see. Eventually, you're going to meet someone who will turn your world upside down, and then you'll understand.''

He leaned forward, so frustrated he could spit. ''Understand what?''

''That you don't need to understand.''

He raised his hands as if to go for her throat and growled at her. ''You are the most obstinate woman.''

''I'm a cupcake, and you know it.''

''Fine. You're a cupcake. I just hope you know that when I end up old and alone, a bitter, senile octogenarian, you'll be to blame.''

''Yes, dear. So tell me about her.''

He smiled, remembering his meeting with Jessica, the look of her. ''She's a fine-looking woman. Kind of exotic, but in an old-fashioned way. Like a Renaissance painting.''

''Reubens?''

He shook his head. ''No, more like a Botticelli. Complete with red hair, pale skin. Damn.''

''Okay, so we know you like that part of her, now what about the part above the neck?''

''That part's just as intriguing.''

Her eyebrows went up. ''Really?''

He reached over to the little hand-painted table where, next to the fruit bowl, he found a lemon muffin. Homemade, of course. His mother loved to cook what she grew. After an enormous bite and some coffee, he said, ''She's bright. Running a media campaign for a major new cosmetics firm. She's all career, and determined to top out at CEO.''

"And that's intriguing how?"

"Come on, Mom. Not everyone can be as well balanced as you."

"No, but they can be a little balanced. I already assumed she had no real life. If she had, surely she wouldn't have had to hire the likes of you."

"Yeah, she's pretty focused. But that works in my favor. I figure she's not going to get coy with me, or have a secondary agenda. I'll ask. She'll answer."

"And what if she doesn't have the answers?"

"I'll keep looking. But I'll have tried."

Colleen sighed, as she ran her hand through her softly graying hair. "We always encouraged you to go out into the field, to learn from experience. Just don't let your hopes get too high, okay?"

"Look, even I know there aren't going to be pat answers. But there are going to be clues. Directions. Hints. I think, if I can just talk about it with no games, I can move to the next level."

"Don't you need someone on this level to be able to move on to the next?"

"I'm hoping it will help me find the kind of woman I can move on with. Even you have to admit I've done a lousy job in my previous selections."

"Oh, honey. Lousy is being kind. But that's mostly because you let your little head do your thinking for you."

"It's a good thing I ceased being embarrassed by you years ago."

"I know. And I appreciate your indulgence."

"So, you'll take care of Mercy?"

"The cat hates me, but yes, I will."

He leaned over, kissed her cheek, then went back to his muffin. "Great."

"And you'll tell me what you've learned?"

"Sure, why not?"

"Oh, goody."

He stood. "I've got to run. If you need me, I'll have the cell."

"Okay, sweetheart. Take some muffins."

He grinned. "I planned to."

"Take some vegetables, too."

"In your dreams."

He squeezed her hand and headed for the kitchen, where up above the sink was a picture he'd taken years ago, of his father and mother. They looked so damn happy.

THE HOTEL SUITE was straight out of a Fred Astaire–Ginger Rogers movie. It was all silver, white and high deco, right down to the crown molding. Huge by any standard, but especially for Manhattan, it had to be priced to the sky. If she'd made the reservations, she'd have been several floors down in a single, but that wouldn't have been the perfect setting for a seduction, would it?

Owen definitely had a screw loose, and for the first time since she'd met with Dan, she felt fine about the devil's bargain she'd gotten herself into.

Her basic premise still held true—that if Owen saw she was involved, witnessed it with his own eyes, he'd back the hell off. What was new to the equation was Dan's "quest," and worse, her attraction to the man.

She waited while the bellman put her big suitcase on the stand, then she tipped him outrageously, fully expecting to have to tax the hotel staff to the limit during her stay. He thanked her, gave a slight bow and left her to unpack.

Once alone, she fought the temptation to lie down on the puffy white comforter, to bury her head in the assemblage of pillows and sleep for three days. Instead, she unzipped her bag and went methodically through the contents, storing them in her typically organized fashion. Halfway through the job, she remembered that she was going to be sharing the space. Not only did that make her pause, it led her to open the door to the minibar and pull out a small bottle of Chardonnay.

Sharing a room with a total stranger. That had to be right up near the top of her own personal list of idiotic moves. Okay, so Glen vouched for him, but what did that mean? This was the most important week of her life, and she couldn't afford to move her eye from the ball. So what did she do? Hire the most attractive man she'd met in years to pretend to be her lover. No distraction there. No, sir.

The problem was, he fit her criteria to a tee. Which was unprecedented. She'd never seen a man who had it all: the looks, the brains, the wit, the strong hands, the taste in clothes. Her only hope was getting to know him. No way he was everything he purported to be. Impossible.

He was undoubtedly narcissistic. Given his quest, probably chauvinistic, too. All she had to do was play it cool until he let his true colors shine, and voila, the problem would be solved.

It'd better be solved.

She poured her wine into one of the crystal glasses set on a silver tray by the wet bar, then sank down into the white-satin chair next to the window. Her view was of Central Park, but she stared without seeing it as she thought of the daunting tasks in front of her.

Tomorrow started the festivities, beginning with a makeover party for ten lucky radio listeners, to be held at Bloomingdale's. All using New Dawn cosmetics, of course. Tomorrow night was the grand-opening party at the Panorama, the newest and most highly sought-after nightclub in the city.

Then there was the dessert-and-jazz party at the Rainbow Room, an evening cruise on the Hudson River, Geocaching in Central Park, and finally, the banquet right here at the hotel. By the end of this little adventure, she'd be ready for the funny farm, but in the meantime, she had to make sure the media was happy, the models showed up and acted like civilized human beings, the celebrities were catered to, and that every detail of every event was taken care of with no muss and utterly no fuss.

Thank God for Marla. And Marla's troops. Jessica was really lucky to have them. And she mustn't forget that every event had a professional planner in charge of it. Which did comfort, but didn't assuage, the final responsibility, which lay directly on her shoulders. Sure, it was Owen who signed the checks, but everyone in the business knew who was really in charge.

This was her ticket. Her chance to soar. If she blew it, she doubted her career could recover. If she succeeded, she'd be well on her way to the dream.

Which meant there was no room at all for Dan in any other capacity but paid help. Maybe it wasn't too late to tell him she'd changed her mind. She could call up an escort service and hire some lovely hunk of maleness, preferably someone gay, who would be silent for a fee.

She'd put Dan's phone number in her purse, and as she rose to fetch it, there was a knock at the door.

She crossed the white marble floor, then looked through the peephole. Owen. Dammit. After a deep breath, she opened the door, but not very far. "Owen, hi. What's up?"

He smiled at her. That goofy, love-struck grin that made her want to bitch-slap him silly. "How do you like it?"

"The suite is fabulous, but too extravagant. My God, it must cost a fortune."

"Two fortunes." He stepped closer, clearly expecting her to let him inside. "But you're worth it."

"Thank you," she said, using the one technique that had merited any success. A simple response. No embellishment. Owen had some difficulty coming up with original thought.

"We need to talk about tomorrow."

"We do?"

He nodded. She spied little drops of perspiration beading his forehead where his hairline used to be. At least he didn't do the comb-over thing. That would have been the icing on the cake. As it was, he wasn't bad-looking. Slightly pudgy, not too tall. She used to find him vaguely handsome, until he'd changed from Dr. Jekyll to Mr. Horny Hyde. "Yeah, you know. The details."

She gave him her most reassuring grin. "That's why you hired me, Owen. To take care of the details. So you don't have to worry in the least. The makeovers are going to be a smash, and so is the opening party. All you have to do is show up at Panorama at eight tomorrow night. Which reminds me, I have to go make a couple of calls—"

"Jess," he said, planting his foot firmly in the door and using his shoulder to ease himself in. "I have some concerns about the party."

She wanted to shove him right back outside, but thought better of it. This would all come to an end soon, and then she wouldn't have to worry anymore. In the meantime, however, she wanted to maximize the distance between them, so she closed the door and walked over to the wet bar. "Soda?"

"No thanks," he said, his glee at gaining entrance far too evident on his face.

"You have concerns?"

He immediately adopted an air of thoughtfulness as his gaze shifted to the bedroom door. "What's our TV coverage on this thing?"

She'd told him before. Written him memos. But she said none of that. "*Entertainment Tonight, E!, Access Hollywood,* MTV, VH1, and three cable shows."

He nodded. "Good, good. And what about celebrities? Are they all verified?"

"We're sending twelve limos, but most of the crowd is arriving on its own."

"Who, exactly?"

She bit back a sigh. "Julia Roberts, Keanu Reeves, Reese Witherspoon, Sarah Michelle Gellar, Freddie Prinze Jr., Nicole Kidman, and oodles more. Should I ask Marla to come up with the list?"

"No," he said too quickly. "That's great. Just great."

"But it won't be just great if I can't make the calls I need to, so…" She headed toward the door. He didn't follow.

"I'm sure the calls can wait a few minutes."

"No, Owen, they can't."

The expression on his face changed again. This time to lovelorn puppy. "Jess, can't you see what a team we make? Isn't it obvious?"

"Yes, absolutely. The next week will prove it. We're going to make New Dawn a household name."

He walked toward her, holding his hands out as if he meant to grasp her, which was simply out of the question. Only, he was blocking her easy exit. In order to get around him, she'd have to practically leap over the chaise. "That's not the partnership I'm talking about."

"There is no other partnership, Owen."

"But there can be. Should be."

"You have a partner already."

He shook his head as he took those last steps, angling himself so that now she truly was caught. His right hand touched her forearm. "I don't. Honestly. I've told you before. Ellen is a great mom—"

"*I've* got a partner, Owen."

He stopped. Blinked. Kept his hand right where it was. "What?"

"A partner. A man. I have someone in my life."

First, a flash of hurt, then confusion, quickly followed by doubt. "What are you talking about? You don't date."

"I don't talk about dating."

"You're always at the office."

"No, I'm not. I do have a life. Which is private. But there is someone, and it's serious."

Doubt became out-and-out disbelief. "Who?"

"You don't know him."

"What's his name?"

"Not that it matters, but Dan."

"Dan what?"

The annoyance factor was starting to shift into the furious factor. "Crawford."

"Never heard of him."

"Exactly."

"How did you meet?"

"In school. Ages ago."

"And he just showed up again?"

"That's right. He showed up, and the old flames were rekindled."

Owen finally removed his hand from her arm. "Where does he live?"

She stepped back, grabbed the door handle. "I don't see why that's important."

"It is."

"Why?"

Flustered, he looked around the room as if searching for a clue. "Because I care about you. I don't want you to get in with the wrong sort of man."

"He's not. I assure you. He's a very good man, and I care about him."

"This is pretty sudden."

"Actually, it's not."

"Marla knows about him?"

"No, she doesn't."

His mouth thinned. "Why not?"

God, she wanted to throttle him. "Because it's no one's business. I keep my private life private."

"Right."

"Owen, I have to make some phone calls."

"Uh-huh. Dan Crawford, right? What does he do? Is he in marketing?"

"No, he's not." She opened the door. "Please, if you don't mind. I have work to do."

He made a move toward the door, but before he crossed the threshold, he turned to face her, his determination a bit daunting. "Come on, Jess. Don't forget who you're talking to. I know your hours. I've called you at home at 3:00 a.m., at five. You're either there or at work, or in transit. So where did this private life come from? What, did you rub a bottle and he popped out?"

"No," came a voice from just behind her. "She won me in a poker game."

She whirled around to see Dan, bags in hand, staring past her. She'd never been so grateful to see anyone.

The small gurgle behind her made her turn back to Owen, who looked decidedly greenish.

"Owen McCabe," she said, "this is Dan Crawford. "Dan, this is Owen."

Dan put down his bag, put one arm around her shoulder and swung her into his arms. Then he kissed her. Kissed her as if he owned her. Kissed her until she thought her knees would give out.

Not just lips to lips, but teasing tongue, hot breath, intimacy that made her clench her fists so she wouldn't push him away. Then his tongue slipped between her teeth, and he was inside her. This man she didn't know. Her hired escort. And, good God almighty, her entire body went ballistic. Everything from goose bumps to hard nipples to curling toes.

She heard Owen cough, but that was somewhere out there, and she was busy. She tasted him back, rubbed her unclenched hand over the breadth of his shoulders.

Finally, when he was well and truly finished, he let her go. She gasped for breath, sure her face was aflame, her arousal as clear as the blush.

Dan smiled too knowingly, turned to her boss and grabbed his hand. "Nice to meet you, Owen. Jessica has told me a lot about you."

HOW TO IMPRESS A WOMAN

Wine her and dine her. Listen to her. Laugh with her. Buy her flowers. Go shopping with her. Don't stop reminding her she is beautiful. Console her when she is down. Rejoice with her when she is up. Read romantic poetry to her. Tell her you love her.

HOW TO IMPRESS A MAN

Arrive naked. Bring beer.

Source: Borja, Greg "How to Impress a Woman"
http://www.buzzle.com/

4

DAN FOCUSED his whole attention on Owen McCabe. Not just because he wanted to gauge the man's reaction to his rather spectacular introductory move, but because he didn't dare think about that kiss.

Holy shit. He hadn't expected anything like that. Not that he hadn't had great kisses before, but this was…he wasn't sure what it was. Maybe because he knew he was going to be spending so much time with her, talking about such intimate things. Or maybe because he'd been thinking so much about her. On the other hand, it might just be that the woman turned him on like a light switch.

Owen's face had shifted from bright red to a subtle pink, but his eyes were still wide with shock, and his hand, still in Dan's, gripped him so hard it hurt. Dan coughed, and that got Owen to let go. "I'm just glad I get to be around for the big doin's," Dan said, all bonhomie and good grace.

"Around?"

"Didn't Jessica tell you? I'm going to stay for the campaign. Lend a hand when I can. Watch my girl in her hours of glory." He turned a beaming smile on Jessica, who looked just a little freaked. He eased his arm around her shoulder and gave her a squeeze. "It's going to be great."

Owen looked as if he'd been stabbed repeatedly with a small knife. "You're staying the whole week?"

"Yep. But don't worry. I won't interfere. I've been given the rules, which I intend to obey to the letter."

The pink in Owen's cheeks got a little darker. "But I, uh…"

"Jessica has told me how great you've been, and how much she's learned from you. I'm impressed."

Again, Owen blinked. Rapidly. "Impressed."

"You bet. She's so damn bright, I never expected her to find a boss who could keep her on her toes. But you sure have."

Now it was Jessica's turn to clear her throat. "Owen was just leaving," she said, "because I have calls to make. You know, uh, business calls."

"Right," Dan said. "Well, great meeting you, Owen." He picked up his bag. "I'm sure we'll see a lot of each other. I look forward to it."

Owen's mouth opened, but nothing came out.

Dan didn't wait for words. He just walked to the door, held it open for Jessica, then closed it behind them.

As for Jessica, she walked straight to a white chair by the window, picked up a glass and swallowed the contents.

"Pretty slick, eh?" he said, heading toward the closet. "I think he bought it."

"I think we almost had to call the paramedics."

Dan chuckled. "I figured why not go for it? Give him both barrels right from the get-go. Give him something to chew on while he sits it out in his suite."

Jessica studied him with a bit more wariness than he cared for. "I don't imagine he'll need another demonstration that's quite so vivid."

"Maybe not. But as you've said, he isn't one to grasp the subtleties."

Her eyes widened. "That was about as subtle as a Sherman tank."

"And fun, too. How about that?"

Jessica put down her glass and crossed her arms. She looked terrific in her cream jacket and slim skirt. Those high heels made her seem taller, which, he supposed, was the point for her, but they made him itch to run his fingers down the long line of her calf.

She did do a pretty good job of looking stern and no-nonsense, he had to give it to her. "About the fun part," she said, her tone keeping pace with her scowl. "This is a job, and I have no intention of letting it get even the slightest bit out of hand. If it becomes necessary for you to put on a show of affection, I insist that you take the minimum step, not the maximum, and that you always keep in mind that it means nothing. Absolutely nothing."

He nodded, trying to match her seriousness. "I'm sorry. I shouldn't have made any reference to my enjoyment level. It was unprofessional. I've never been a paid escort before, so you'll have to forgive me. I'll do better in the future."

He could tell she wasn't sure if he was mocking her, and for a moment he thought she might really let into him, but she didn't. She just uncrossed her arms and went to the coffee table, where she got her phone from her purse. "Feel free to put your things away. This couch opens up into a bed, so you can plan accordingly." Then she started punching in a phone number.

He took her at her word and unpacked. He'd brought a wide selection of clothes, from city casual to black-tie, not knowing what kind of events he'd be expected to attend. When he stashed his night kit in the bathroom, he thought it prudent to keep the condoms tucked away with his razor and shaving cream.

When all was stashed, he poured himself a soda from the bar, got his notes from his briefcase and sat down at the corner desk.

He listened to Jessica for a few minutes while he pretended to read. And while the conversation about overtime for models didn't interest him in the least, the way she carried herself did.

Glen had been very accurate when he'd described her as a powerhouse. She conducted business from a position of strength and confidence, and even though he only heard her side of the negotiations, he could tell she was going to get her way. There was no doubt in her mind, and it was only a matter of time before she'd convinced the model's rep of the same thing.

Good. His instincts had been right on. This wasn't a woman who was going to get all shy and giggly when he asked her about clitoral stimulation. He studied his notes, scanning the outline he'd made the night before. It wasn't complete, but he figured the dialogue would suggest other topics and tangents.

He wished they could start right now. Looking at her again, leaning back against the satin chair, her auburn hair shimmering against the white background, her skirt mid-thigh, her ankles crossed, he wondered what he would ask her first. He'd led with the most obvious question of all, at least in his notes. "What do you want from a man?" But now that seemed the wrong approach. Because if he asked her something like that, she'd give him a quick answer, undoubtedly correct, but limited in thought and perspective. By the time he got to that question, he wanted her to have lived with him for a while, with the concepts he was exploring. He wanted an answer that was as complex as the woman before him, nothing less.

So what would start the dialogue? He was hoping that her answers would provoke and startle him, get him thinking in new arenas.

He'd read all the books that were currently in vogue, but none of them had given him precisely what he was looking for.

When he'd been in the few relationships that had lasted any time at all, there had been something illusive, something "other" about the women he cared for. Something that had doomed them, he was convinced, from the start.

His father had clearly understood his mother, because they had been like two sides of the same coin. They had a shared language, reserved only for the two of them. Unfortunately, he hadn't thought of asking his dad about his secret while he'd had the chance. Not that he hadn't talked to other married men, but they'd all said pretty much the same thing: listen to her. Put her first. Don't try to solve all her problems, just pay attention and only make suggestions when asked. Which was all fine and good, but it didn't get to the essential mystery. At least not for him.

It had occurred to him that while he might be bright as hell when it came to computer software and basic research, maybe the missing ingredient was in him, not in the information he was lacking. But this experiment was designed to bring that flaw to the fore, should that be the case. He wouldn't be pleased to know it, but at least he'd stop trying so damn hard.

No, this was worthwhile, and he couldn't do anything to muck it up. Jessica had all the qualities of a perfect research subject, and he was privileged to have the opportunity.

So the best thing to do was forget about any libidinous side trips. This was a field study; no fraternizing with the natives.

"Just to warn you," Jessica said, standing and putting her phone back in her purse. "My assistant is on her way up. I'll introduce you, but she won't need any convincing. Okay?"

"Right. I'll be the perfect gentleman."

"That's fine. We're going to be a while, though, so if you have something else you want to do."

"Nope. As long as I'm not in the way."

She headed for the bar and got herself a soda, loading up her glass with ice. "I don't think you will be, but please don't take offense if I ask you to take a walk or something. This is all new to me, too.''

''No problem.''

She sipped some soda, then got a tan leather briefcase from the bedroom before she settled once more on the white chair. A moment later, she was taking notes, and had forgotten him.

He watched her for a long time as she worked. He liked her hands, the way they were so small, but so definite in their every move. Her nails, while polished a nearly flesh-colored pink, were short and serviceable. Like everything about her, they were meant to do the job, not to interfere. Unlike so many women he'd known, she wasn't constantly flipping back her hair, or tossing it aside. Although her rich auburn locks were smooth and silky, and moved along with her head, there were no strays in her eyes, or on her cheeks.

Her makeup was like that, too. Subdued. Practical. He knew a little about that, having lived with Tamara. She'd always gone for extravagant makeup, the darker, the more dramatic, the better. But that was very high maintenance, whereas Jessica looked as if she could get out of the bathroom in ten minutes. Of course, he could be wrong. Maybe looking that natural took hours, but he doubted it. She had things to accomplish, none of which would happen until she was on her way.

What made her so driven? He wanted to know everything about her background. Only child? That would be his guess. That or eldest. But he'd bank on only. Successful father, someone to live up to. She probably didn't have a lot of friends, as those were distractions, too. No pets. Okay, maybe fish, but then no. He doubted she'd want to worry about anything like that.

The only other woman he'd known well that was as driven had been Kathleen Butler, an arbitrage banker he'd met at Mulloney's one night. They'd played pool, and although he was decent, she'd kicked his ass every game. Then she'd taken him to her apartment where they'd had really kinky sex. She'd wanted to be dominated, tied up. Owned. He'd gone along with it, and in fact had enjoyed himself a lot, but he hadn't called her again. The domination thing was fun for a night, but not a steady diet.

He wondered if Jessica would be like that. In charge totally when it came to work, and wanting none of that in bed. The idea appealed, but maybe that's because anything to do with sex and Jessica appealed.

He jotted down some notes about it, fully intending to ask her.

By the time he'd finished, there was a knock at the door, and Jessica opened it to reveal another redhead. This one was younger by several years, just out of college, he guessed. She was pretty, with a quirky little mouth and enormous eyes. The look she gave him was all wonder and curiosity, but it didn't compare to the look she gave her boss.

He stood up for the introductions. Marla shook his hand, but her gaze was still on Jessica. Talk about dumbfounded. Okay, so what Glen had said was true—Jessica didn't date. Or at the very least she kept her private life private.

"Can I get you a drink?" he asked, remembering his manners. Even though it wasn't Owen, he was still supposed to be the dutiful boyfriend.

"Sure," Marla said. "I think I need one."

"Soda? Wine?"

"Soda, please. Wine later. Work and all. I can't afford to get all woogy."

"Woogy?"

She nodded. "All alcohol brain. There's so much going on. Tomorrow there are the makeovers, and then all the models and stuff. Busy, busy."

"So I heard. You must be excited."

She smiled beguilingly, the lovely pink of her cheeks aglow. "I am. I'm learning so much."

"She's saving my ass," Jessica said. "And I'd love to go on and on about it, but I think having a good night's sleep is in our best interest, so what do you say we get to it?"

"Absolutely," Marla said, and she ensconced herself on the couch, folding her legs beneath her.

Dan got her a soda, put it within her reach, then settled himself back at the desk. He intended to take notes, think more about the whole domination thing, but he got wrapped up in the dynamic of the two women, and didn't move until 9:40 p.m., when Jessica called it a night. The hours had sped by, and he'd learned a thing or two about his subject. Mostly, that he liked her style. A lot.

JESSICA CLOSED the door behind Marla, and fought the urge to rest her head against the cool wood. She was tired. Not just because this was D day minus one, but because of the man sitting in the corner.

She'd had to use all her powers of concentration to ignore him. She never got distracted. A damn hurricane could be blowing outside, and she'd never raise an eyebrow. But he'd pulled at her ever since he'd walked down the hall.

She'd thought about asking him to leave, but figured she'd get over the awareness with time. It hadn't happened. She was just as interested in him now as she had been, more so now that they were alone.

What had he been writing? And how could he have sat and listened so quietly for all those hours? She couldn't imagine he was interested in New Dawn cosmetics.

This whole project of his confused her, and his behavior tonight hadn't cleared up a thing. He seemed like a very bright man. In fact, after doing a little more checking up on him since their initial meeting, she'd discovered he was brilliant. A self-made millionaire, owner of a consulting firm that designed revolutionary computer systems, currently in use with, among others, the FBI, the IRS and the DOD. Not too shabby.

She turned to see him stretching, arching his back so his shirt rode up, revealing a tiny little patch of skin by his belt. She closed her eyes, although she couldn't have said why, and when she opened them again, he'd brought his arms down. "I still don't get it," she said. "I can't imagine what questions you think I can answer for you."

"That's okay. I can. I have a lot of them written down in my little notebook."

"For example?"

He shook his head. "Nope. Not yet. Right now, I think the important thing is food. I'm starving and you must be, too."

She looked at the bedroom with longing. That's what she really wanted. Sleep. But he was right, she hadn't eaten since her power bar this morning. "I could use some dinner."

"Great. Why don't we just go downstairs. They have great steaks and a good wine cellar at Gigot."

"That sounds fine. I want to freshen up first, though."

"You go ahead. I'll call down."

She went to the rest room, a little startled to see his things next to hers on the counter. It was only a leather shaving kit, but still. She tried to remember the last time she'd shared a bathroom with a guy. College. And not that often.

Her gaze went to her reflection. She didn't look as frazzled as she felt. The important thing was not to let this arrangement get to her. He was just a hired hand. Someone doing a job. She'd done research in college, and she understood how it worked. He'd ask, she'd answer, and the rest of the time, she'd work. Simple, and yet...

She was so *aware* of him. Of his broad shoulders, his slim hips. The way his hair fell across his forehead. That nose of his that was too big, and yet exactly right. The way he kissed.

She sighed, slumping her shoulders and staring blindly at the sink. That kiss had knocked her for a loop. It had caught her completely off guard. Not just that he'd kissed her, but that she had reacted so fiercely. Her toes had curled. For God's sake, that didn't happen to her. Not ever. And it wasn't going to happen again. This was her moment, and nothing and no one was going to get in the way. If she had to, she'd fire him.

HE ORDERED the 1999 E. Guigal Châteauneuf-du-Pape, which Jessica happened to know was the Wine of the Year for 2002 according to *Wine Spectator.* This to go with the filet mignon she'd ordered, and the T-bone he'd asked for.

Normally, she wasn't big on steak, but tonight it felt right. As did the small salad with the unbelievably good balsamic vinaigrette, the roasted red potatoes and the sourdough bread that was way too good. Of course, the wine made everything sheer bliss. It was perfect. The meal, the atmosphere, which was dark but not too dark, cozy, quiet. The waiters didn't hover, but were never out of reach. And she even liked the painting on the wall behind Dan. It was modern, no real subject, but nice.

They'd talked a lot about his mother, of all things, during the meal. Jessica had heard of Colleen Crawford, had even read articles by her. It seemed the two of them had a terrific relationship, and according to Dan, his parents' marriage had been ideal. But it begged the question "Why don't you ask her these questions that have you so confused?"

"She won't answer me."

"What?"

"She won't. She tells me I have to learn some things through experience."

"But you don't believe her."

"I don't disbelieve her, but I think she's been spoiled by her own relationship. I don't think she sees the dilemma."

"Frankly, I don't think I do, either."

"You will, the more we talk."

"Don't be so sure. I'm not terribly bright when it comes to men. I've never been in love or anything remotely close to it."

His eyebrows came down for a moment, and he sipped some more of his wine. "I don't think that'll matter."

"No?"

"My questions are about you. About what you want. What you need."

"I can tell you that in about two sentences."

"I'm sure. But I hope you won't. I want you to answer my questions in the order I'm going to ask them. Not before."

"Fair enough."

He smiled.

She ate the last piece of bread on her plate. After she'd swallowed, she tapped the table. "Well?"

"What?"

"Ask."

"Oh, no. Not yet."

"Why not?"

"Because I'm having a really good time."

She laughed. "And questions will spoil it?"

He shrugged. "Maybe. I don't know."

"Just how offensive are these questions?"

It was his turn to laugh. "Not at all. Although, they are personal."

"So I'd assumed."

"We'll start later."

"When, later? I'm exhausted. All I want now is bed. I have to be up at five."

"Which means I have to be up at five, right?"

She shook her head. "Nope. Tomorrow morning is makeover day. I'll be at Bloomingdale's. Owen won't be."

"So when do I report for duty?"

"Tomorrow evening. It's the big opening party. I'm afraid it's black-tie."

"No problem. I'm all set."

"Okay, then. Just be available from about five on."

"Yes, ma'am."

She knew he would handle the party well. He was every bit the sophisticate, although not in the least obnoxious about it. The conversation had flowed with surprising ease. But still. "No, it's not going to work," she said.

He immediately sat forward. "What?"

"I'm never going to get to sleep wondering what the hell you're going to ask me. So you have to. Ask. At least one question. Dinner's about done, so it can't ruin much."

He leaned back, not looking pleased. "All right. If you insist."

"I do."

He looked down for a long moment, long enough for her to grab her fork so she could stab him with it if he didn't for Pete's sake say something. Then he lifted his head and his gaze met hers. "Do you like being tied up for sex?"

Five things you'll NEVER hear one woman say to another woman:

1. *Oh, look, that woman and I have the same dress on! I think I'll go introduce myself!*

2. *His new girlfriend is thinner and better-looking than I am, and I'm happy for them both.*

3. *I'm sick of dating doctors and lawyers! Give me a good old-fashioned waiter with a heart of gold any day!*

4. *He talks our relationship to death! It's making me crazy!*

5. *Why can't I find a guy who'll have a wild carefree night of sex and then just go his separate way for once?*

Source: Thompson, Dave "Things You'll Never Hear"
http://www.ijmc.com/

5

JESSICA STARED at Dan, the words he'd spoken echoing in her head. He sat languidly against the dark brown leather, his right arm on the seat, his left still on the table. "Do I *what?*"

"Like being tied up for sex?" He leaned forward, moving both hands to his wineglass, his eyes dancing with the light from the flickering-candle centerpiece. "You know, being dominated. Letting yourself be taken, giving the control over to your partner."

She took her own wine and drank it all, then put the crystal goblet down carefully. "You said you wanted to ask questions about women. Not about sex."

He shook his head. "Sex is part of it. A big part of it. Of course, it's true, I hadn't planned on opening with this question, but evidently it was on my mind. So, what the hell."

"What the hell?" She crossed her legs, folded her hands on her lap. "I know I agreed to be candid, but for God's sake, Dan, this is a bit much."

"Oh," he said, surprise evident in his voice and his expression. "I thought you understood. It's all going to be personal. Intimate. That's the point."

There was still a bit more wine in the bottle, and she poured it all in her glass. If it wasn't for the day she faced tomorrow, she would have asked for another bottle.

"I'm not asking to make you uncomfortable. Honestly. I just need to understand you."

"And whether or not I like being tied up is going to give you special insight?"

He nodded. "Maybe not special, but insight, definitely."

"Why would you even think—"

"Because you're so strong," he said. "I watched you work today, and you're a woman who likes to be in control. At least in the workplace. Which made me think that in other areas, you might find it a relief to give up that control."

She'd heard that, herself. Actually read about it. Mostly in regards to powerful men, who went to expensive sex clubs where a dominatrix would put them through their paces. After another sip of wine and a deep breath, she met Dan's gaze. "Well, I'll tell you, Dan. I've never been tied up for sex, so I can't honestly say I like it or I don't."

"Ever thought about it?"

"No."

"Really?"

"Now that's not going to work. Either we're doing this thing, which I now doubt, or we're not. If we do proceed, you're going to have to believe me, or what's the point?"

"No. I didn't mean I doubted your word. I meant—"

"Okay, then. And yes, really. I've never thought about it."

"I see."

"You sound disappointed."

"I'm not. Well, maybe a little."

She laughed, more out of surprise than anything. "You're a very unusual person. You know that, right?"

"Unusual? That's a nice way to put it. But yes, I know. I've been that way forever. Probably because of the way I was brought up."

"Which was?"

"My parents didn't believe in traditional education. I didn't go to school."

"I don't understand."

"I was homeschooled. But even that wasn't done in the traditional way. My parents were devotees of a man named John Holt. He believed that children are sponges, and that curiosity is innate. Given the opportunity, kids will explore every subject they can. But most kids aren't afforded the luxury of being able to learn freely. I was."

"How did you decide what to explore?"

"Whatever caught my interest. I liked bugs, so I went out and caught all kinds of bugs. I read books on entomology. I went to museums in Africa, Asia and right here in New York. So I know a lot about bugs."

"But that supposes you knew how to read. That you knew what to look up."

"Right. My folks taught me to read and write. Very early, evidently. And I went to libraries and museums before I could walk."

"And that's how you learned everything? What if you'd decided you didn't like math?"

"That's the whole point. Anything can be interesting if it's presented with passion. I saw early that money was a powerful tool, so learning how to count it came as a natural consequence."

"But there were subjects in school I hated."

"I'll bet your teachers had a great deal to do with it. Remember, the key is passion. It's infectious. You want to participate when someone's having a blast. My parents made sure I was exposed to people who loved what they did."

"My God. How did they know you'd be well rounded? What about college?

He smiled. "I didn't go. The way I see it, I'm still in the university. Remember, learning isn't really about rote memorization, not even close. It's about understanding. Not that I understand everything I tackle, but I get close. I mean, I get the basics of quantum physics, but that's it. On the other hand, I know quite a bit about computer software.''

"So I read."

He raised a eyebrow. "Read?"

"You didn't think I was going to let you stay in my room without doing some research of my own, did you?"

"I didn't think about it, but now that you mention it, smart move. What did you discover?"

"That you've got a highly successful software consulting business, and that you weren't kidding when you said you didn't need my money."

"That's it? All you found out was about my business life?"

"I looked on the Internet, not into a crystal ball."

His laugh made her smile. The conversation made her dizzy. He was like no one she'd ever met. The sex question had thrown her for a loop, and she still wasn't sure she wanted to bare that much of her life to a stranger, but on the other hand, my God. He was fascinating. She hadn't been fascinated by a man in…forever.

"Well, next time, go beyond Google. I'm in there."

"What would I find?"

He shook his head. "Nope. I'm not going to tell you. I don't want to be the only one who's surprised during our time together."

"I think that ship has sailed. I'm surprised. Trust me."

He leaned over so his mouth came very close to her ear. So close, she could feel his warm breath. "You ain't seen nothin' yet," he whispered.

"No," she said, her voice just as soft, although she couldn't fathom why. "I imagine I haven't." After she cleared her throat, uncrossed her legs and checked the time, she turned to him again. "But let's try not to shock me out of my wits, shall we? This week is awfully important."

"I can't make any promises," he said. "But I'll try."

"Thank you."

"It's time to hit the sack. Unless you want dessert?"

She shook her head. "I need sleep. As much as I can steal."

"Then let me take care of this posthaste."

He was true to his word, and in short order they were back at the suite Owen had so kindly provided. The first thing she saw when she turned on the light was a basket of inordinate size sitting on the coffee table. She crossed the room and plucked the card from the wrapping. She read:

Jessica, I loved the gag. Let's talk. Breakfast tomorrow before Bloomingdale's? I'll be in the coffee shop at six.

The note wasn't signed, but of course she knew who it was from. At least she knew she'd be having breakfast in the suite.

"Cool basket," Dan said. "From Owen?"

"Yep."

"I see chocolate. I see champagne. Excellent."

"What do you mean?"

"He's worried. By the time the party's over tomorrow night, he'll be totally convinced."

"I hope so."

"Trust me."

She tossed the card on the table and looked into Dan's eyes. "You know what's completely weird?"

"What?"

"I do."

MARLA CHECKED her clipboard for the fiftieth time in the last hour. Everything had gone like clockwork at the makeover, which made her very nervous.

All ten of the lucky winners had been coiffed, massaged, facialed and made up with New Dawn cosmetics, and they all looked fabulous. Pictures had been taken, the media had been cooperative, and all in all, the first leg of Operation New Dawn had been a smashing success.

Now, while Jessica was doing her last-minute thing at the Panorama, Marla was in charge of collecting the models and getting them spruced up and prepared for the night's soiree.

No problem. Except, of course, for one thing. In Marla's not-so-humble opinion, the model, no *The Model* who was the star of the campaign wasn't Sheree O'Brien, although she was making almost five million dollars a year as the New Dawn woman. The real star was none other than Shawn Foote. He wasn't as famous as Sheree, but he was much, much better-looking. In fact, he was the single most handsome man on the face of the earth. Marla knew this, because she'd seen a lot of people, and none of them came close to Shawn's gorgeousness.

Just thinking about him made her palms all sweaty, which sucked because she might get to touch him, and she didn't want him going "Ugh" first thing. First impressions, and all.

But, oh, he was so… She sighed. His hair, honey-wheat and thick, tumbled around his face in the sexiest possible way. His brown eyes were sweet and soulful. She sighed. She was going to be a gibbering idiot when she met him, she just knew it.

Checking her watch again, she saw the models were due in, like, two minutes. They had taken over half the salon at the hotel, and cordoned it off. A whole lot of lookie-loos were standing outside the barricade, waiting to see what was going on. Also some paparazzi, but she wasn't worried. Publicity was the name of this game.

All she had to do was not trip or throw up or something.

Act like a professional. Act like Jessica. She could do it. At least she could try.

A limousine pulled up under the awning, and a uniformed bellman went to the door. Marla's heart started thumping in her chest and she wiped her hands on her skirt. Pasting on a smile, she walked to the curb, but it was just Sheree. Of course, the throng went a little nuts, and the flashbulbs exploded all around, but she'd met the supermodel before, and Sheree even remembered her name. Marla escorted her to the waiting stylists, made sure she had coffee, then skedaddled back outside.

Two more models showed up, and Marla hustled them inside, and then, it happened. *He* arrived. The only male model, there to show off Daybreak cologne, he stepped out of his limo wearing worn jeans, a Joe Boxer T-shirt and scuffed Skechers. Her heart skipped, jumped, leapt as he turned her way and smiled. Oh, God! That smile. That face. That hair. She couldn't take it. She was going to die, right here, and that would be okay because Shawn had smiled at her as if she was a real person or something.

"You must be Marla," he said.

His voice. It was just as she'd imagined. Soft, low, perfect. She managed a nod.

"Great to meet you. I'm Shawn." He held out his hand.

She panicked. Sweat. Ugh. But she couldn't wipe it again. Not while he stood there. So she just swallowed hard and stuck it out there.

His grip was gentle, but not wussy. He hesitated for just a few seconds. She knew because she counted every heartbeat. Then he let her go, at least her hand. Not her gaze. That he held, and she was lost. Lost.

"Where to?" he asked.

"I don't… Oh. Uh, this way." She spun around, almost losing her footing, but she didn't fall, thank God, and she somehow walked him past all the photographers and gawkers until he was inside the salon.

Terry, the lucky dog, was going to put on Shawn's makeup for all the pictures and stuff. There were going to be tons of TV cameras and photographers. But he didn't seem to mind. He just sat down, grinned and said, "Have at it."

Marla watched as Terry put a big cape over his body, then ran her fingers through his hair.

That was it. All Marla could stand. If she watched for another second she would expire from the sheer magnificence of it all.

She tore her gaze from the mirror, then from the back of his head. She forced herself to take a step, then another until she was around the corner. She slumped against the wall, desperate to get her breathing back to normal. She still had a lot of work to do. But for the moment, while she recovered, she could think about the way he'd smiled.

She sighed. It was going to be a weird and wonderful week.

1. Why do men get married?
   So they don't have to hold their stomachs in anymore.

2. What are a woman's four favorite animals?
   A mink in the closet, a Jaguar in the garage, a tiger in the bedroom and an ass to pay for it all.

3. How do you get a man to do sit-ups?
   Put the remote control between his toes.

4. What's the difference between men and government bonds?
   Bonds mature.

5. Why are married women heavier than single women?
   Single women come home, see what's in the fridge and go to bed. Married women come home, see what's in bed and go to the fridge.

Source: Thompson, Dave "More Dumb Men Jokes"
http://ijmc.com/

6

DAN LOOKED at himself in the mirror, and straightened his tie. He liked the Armani tux and thought it worth the extravagant price he'd paid. The tailoring was so fine he felt completely at ease and ready for the night ahead.

He expected to find Jessica waiting for him in the living room, but the bedroom door was still closed. She'd gotten home an hour ago, given him a brief report on her day, including Owen's insistence that Dan wasn't really her boyfriend, and then she'd closed herself in to get ready for the gala.

He'd stared at the door for a long time, aware of the urge to walk in on her, to watch her as she dressed. In his mind's eye he'd imagined her sorting out her things, preparing herself layer by layer. Dressed in nothing more than a long royal-blue kimono, she'd passed by on her way to her shower. When she reappeared, her hair was fixed in a sensual updo and her makeup made her blue eyes seem startlingly vivid and her full lips moist and ripe as just-picked strawberries.

She'd disappeared again, leaving him to get dressed, and he'd taken his time. They were to be at the party a full hour before the first guests should arrive so that Jessica could take care of any last-minute details. Marla had called once, and Jessica had taken it in the bedroom. Other than that interruption, he'd been left to his own thoughts, which had gone in one very narrow direction.

Last night, after Jessica had gone to bed, hadn't been a

restful one. The question he'd asked her had tormented him, giving rise to image after image of him tying her to his large four-poster. In some scenarios she was naked, but in most she wore something. A bra and panties, white lace or black. A bustier complete with garter and dark hose, and as he'd tied silk scarves to her graceful ankles, he studied her four-inch stilettos. Still another version had her in business garb, a slim skirt he'd hoisted to the junction of her thighs, the better to spread her legs. Her demure jacket unbuttoned and open, revealing a thin teddy that couldn't hide the hard buds of her nipples.

In each of his mental movies, she'd begun with hesitation and not a little bit of fear. As the scene progressed, he'd toyed with her, teased her into a writhing frenzy of lust and desire. In the end, he imagined her cries of release.

The only way he could get himself to sleep was to vow, quite sincerely, that before he'd said goodbye to Jessica, after this charade had ended, he would have her in his bed. And he would let loose the sensual creature he saw just beyond her cool facade.

Morning had come too quickly, and with it, her departure. After she'd left, he'd gone over his notes. The questions he'd written just the day before no longer felt probing enough. He was after something ephemeral and he wasn't certain yet what tack to take.

The frustration had mounted until he'd had to escape the suite. He'd gone to the hotel gym and worked himself into exhaustion on the treadmill and then on free weights. He followed his regular routine, except at home his run was by the Central Park Pond, and when he did his weights, he didn't do as many reps. His muscles still ached, but pleasantly.

Back at the room, he'd showered, dressed and discovered Jessica had returned to the suite. She had been in the bedroom for an hour now, but she would have to come out soon if they were going to be on time. Jessica struck him as someone who would be appalled at tardiness. He thought about having a drink but he wanted to be on his toes to assess the situation at the party. Later, if things went smoothly, he'd indulge in some champagne, but for now, he poured himself a glass of water and settled on the couch.

He didn't have to wait long. The bedroom door opened, and he stood before he turned. What he saw made him swallow hard. She looked like the woman from his fantasies, all of them, wrapped into one. Her sleeveless gown, a deep scarlet that matched her lips, hugged her bodice, lifting her lush, pale breasts into perfect mounds. After tapering at her waist, the material flowed past her hips to swirl around her feet. He could just see the pointed tip of one shoe, the color an exact match to the dress. Simple, elegant, she was everything beautiful and sinful about a woman. The long curve of her neck, the perfection of her shoulders… "Amazing," he said, his voice rough and quieter than he'd intended, the word inadequate by a mile.

Her lips curled into a slow smile, and her cheeks turned a fetching pink. "Thank you. You're pretty amazing yourself."

He grinned. "This old thing? I wear it to pick apples."

He was rewarded with a laugh. He liked the way her eyes crinkled when she let go like that. He liked a lot about her.

"Are you ready?"

"As I'll ever be."

He held his arm out for her. "The chariot awaits, my lady."

"Chariot, my behind. All I want to do is get through tonight with no major disasters."

"It's going to be an unqualified success," he said as she walked up to him. He hadn't noticed before, but she held a small bag in her right hand, scarlet, to match her shoes, glittering to match the magic of her eyes. "The only problem you're going to have is that all the other women will be green with envy."

She touched his arm softly. "I can't believe you don't understand women. You've certainly mastered the art of flattery."

"You think that was flattery? Wrong. Just stating the facts, like the research stud I am."

She laughed again. "Just do me a favor. Keep Owen off my back tonight. Then I'll call you any kind of stud you want."

He waggled his eyebrows as he led her to the door. "I'm going to hold you to that."

"That's fine, hold me." Her step faltered. "To it," she rushed to add.

He didn't say anything, just enjoyed that he could fluster her. Discretion being the better part of valor, he decided to rescue his maiden from further embarrassment. "Tell me more about Owen. Did he find you?"

Her stride evened as they approached the elevator. "Yes, he did. He laughed a lot, like we were sharing some colossal joke. He asked if you were that gay friend of mine."

"What did you tell him?"

"That I should have mentioned you before, because things were getting pretty serious, but that I work hard at keeping my private life private."

"Nice. And his response?"

"I don't know. I was saved by the bell. Marla called, and I went outside to talk to her."

"Better and better. But have no fear. Tonight we'll end his doubts."

The elevator arrived and she led him inside. A man in a rumpled suit rested against the back of the car and the way he stared at Jessica made Dan want to wash his mind out with soap. Dan positioned himself between Jessica and the lecher, putting his arm around her shoulder as the doors whispered closed.

She looked up at him sharply. "Rehearsing?"

He smiled. "You never know who'll be on the other side of those doors."

She didn't seem convinced, although she didn't move away. "Anyway, about tonight..."

"Yes?"

"What is it you're planning? The star attraction tonight is New Dawn. We're going to have a lot of celebrities and I don't want any of the focus of the evening to be on me. Us."

"My only target audience is Owen."

Her furrowed forehead hadn't smoothed. "Just how vivid is this demonstration going to be?"

"Don't worry. It's going to be great. I may not have gone to college but I do know how to behave among them hoity-toity folks."

She smiled, and he felt her shoulders relax. "I trust you. I think."

"You just concentrate on the work," he said. "I'll take care of the rest."

WHEN THEY GOT to the Panorama, the valet opened the limo door, and Jessica stepped onto the pavement, her gaze automatically checking to make sure that the guard ropes held back the gathering paparazzi on either side of the entrance. The bouncers were impeccably dressed in tuxedos, and the klieg lights were sweeping the night sky. All seemed well, and when Dan took her hand to lead her inside, her nerves eased perceptibly. She'd been to lots of events like this—movie premieres, awards shows, restaurant openings, but she'd never been in charge of anything this large before. She took comfort in the strength of her team and the fact that she'd been obsessive in her attention to detail. However, things could still go wrong.

For whatever reason, Dan's hand made things better. His presence radiated confidence that she was able to tap into. Rationally, she should have been more nervous, not less. God knows he sent her thoughts skidding into the danger zone, but maybe that was the key. A large chunk of her fear was siphoned off into sexual awareness. Sure. It made a world of sense. And at least for tonight, she felt grateful.

Inside, the club looked sensational. Festooned with peach and lavender balloons, custom-made to match the New Dawn colors, She'd been afraid that it would look like a sixteen-year-old's bedroom, but the sophistication of the flowers, the artwork and the sheer drapes made it seem more like something out of a beautiful dream. The decor worked, and when the dance floor was packed and the music filled the air, the atmosphere would transform into something sensual and steamy, exactly what she was going for.

Marla waved from the bar and headed their way. She looked fantastic in her simple black gown. With her hair pinned back by a diamond clip and the small diamond studs in her ears, she seemed radiant.

"Oh, you're so gorgeous!" Marla walked a complete circle around them. "Va-va-voom! Both of you."

"Look who's talking," Dan said. "You're going to have every man in the place begging for a scrap of attention."

Her cheeks got hot pink and she looked at the floor. "Oh, right."

Dan lifted her hand. "Hey," he said very softly.

Marla lifted her gaze, but not her head.

"In a very deserted jungle, deep in Costa Rica, I watched a caterpillar turn into a monarch butterfly. The transformation took my breath away, and when I tried later to tell a friend about the beauty of the butterfly, words failed me.

Now all I would have to do is point to you, and he would understand.''

Marla's blush deepened and her eyes grew moist. "I don't…''

Dan leaned over and kissed her cheek. "Knock 'em dead, gorgeous," he whispered, just loudly enough so that Jessica could hear.

Her attention shifted from her assistant to this odd man she'd hired to be her escort. How could he have known that Marla had been struggling to transform herself from a somewhat geeky youth into a confident young woman? That this dress, this whole approach to her looks was new and untested? That what she needed most was a man, particularly a good-looking, confident man, to affirm that she was beautiful, that she could relax into this new phase of her life?

Marla practically floated away with a vague promise to check into something, leaving Jessica alone with Dan. Well, as alone as one could be while waiters and team members scurried about straightening this and adjusting that. He smiled at her, but not in a self-satisfied, gloating way, which she had sort of expected. He'd made the night for Marla, and most men she knew would have worn that triumph like a trophy.

"May I get you something to drink?" he asked. "Or maybe there's some work I can do? I'm pretty handy with a hammer or even a dish towel.''

Jessica shook her head. "No, thanks. I think we've got it under control, but if you'd like, you can come with me while I do a final check.''

"It would be my pleasure.''

AFTER A GOOD HALF HOUR talking with the deejay, checking on the liquor and the hired staff, Jessica led Dan back into the main room of the club. Marla was stationed at the door, welcoming the first of the guests. From this distance Jessica couldn't see who it was. As they walked across the dance floor, she felt Dan's hand slip from her shoulder to the base of her neck. His long fingers felt warm and a bit ticklish. Her first reaction was to cringe, but she mastered herself quickly. She'd never really thought about all the places a man touched a woman that went beyond casual boundaries. An acquaintance could certainly touch a hand, an arm, even a shoulder. But a touch to the neck or face carried with it an unspoken message: I'm entering into the land of the private, here. You're allowing me to. That means we're more than friends, and if you let my hand linger, it means we're heading for intimacy. Jessica hadn't let anyone into her privacy in years, and she wondered if she'd been on a date with Dan, would she have cringed? Or would she have welcomed his touch?

As it stood now, she couldn't very well shake him off. He was simply doing his job. Making it clear to all and sundry that they were a couple. She didn't dare tell him to back off in case Owen was in sight, because Owen could be anywhere at any time, watching for just this kind of thing. In fact, she slowed her pace, looked up to meet Dan's gaze, and slipped her hand around his waist.

"Hey there," he said.

"You're good at this," she said.

"I've been on dates before."

"This isn't one."

"Not technically, no. But why let a little thing like a pesky, oversexed boss get in the way? I'm going to enjoy every minute of tonight, and I hope you are, too."

"It's not important that I enjoy myself. I can't afford to forget I'm working."

"Who says the two are mutually exclusive? You can be observant, take care of business, and still have a blast."

She stopped him short. "What planet are you from?"

He shook his head, his expression puzzled. "Why on earth would you want a career that isn't fun?"

"Fun? Fun isn't the issue."

"Why not? What better criteria are there?"

"Money, power. You know, the things that make the world go round?"

"So you get off on power, do you?"

"Sure."

"You say that like it's a given."

"It is. Power is what it's all about."

"Why?"

"Come on, Dan. Look around. Those who have the most power win."

"Win what? What's the prize?"

She looked over at the front door. More and more people were arriving, and she shouldn't leave Marla to face the crowd on her own. "Let's talk about prizes later, shall we? I need to get over there."

"Of course. But I'm not going to forget where we were."

"I'm sure you're not."

They reached the entrance and Marla stepped to her side. "Donna Karan is here, and so is Kate Spade. The limos are starting to pile up."

"Great. Do me a favor, go ask Eddy to start the champagne and hors d'oeuvres. Have you seen Owen?"

"He got here a while ago. He asked me where you were."

"I'm sure he'll turn up."

Marla gave Dan a big smile, then headed off for the kitchen. Jessica turned to find Donald Trump at the door with his latest girlfriend. She settled in for a long hour of greetings, aware the whole time that Dan was close by.

When the bulk of the crowd had arrived, Dan led Jessica away from the door into the heart of the party. The music, an eclectic mix by one of the most popular deejays in the city, was just loud enough to make conversation difficult. Drinks and food flowed at the hands of the ever attentive staff, and everyone seemed to be having a hell of a good time. He hoped to make that true for Jessica.

She'd handled the introductions like a pro, but when he touched her he could feel the tension in her muscles. Owen had come by briefly, pretty much ignoring Dan, but the crowd had been such that he had to leave Jessica be. Now that they were out in the open, so to speak, Dan felt sure Owen would make his move.

They were in the middle of the dance floor, Madonna singing a techno-song with a strong beat. Dan grabbed Jessica's hand and spun her around to face him. "Let's dance," he shouted.

She shook her head no, and tried to turn away but he stopped her.

"Come on, one dance. It'll do you good."

She closed the distance between them and he bent at the waist so his ear was near her mouth. "I don't know how."

"Ah," he said. "Then I'll wait for a slow song."

"Dan, I have work to do."

"What work would that be? Everything's going great."

"I need to make sure it continues."

"It will. Look around."

She did, with a slow arc, turning around until she'd seen the whole room.

"See? These people know how to party."

She nodded, but seemed captivated by something in a dark corner. He followed her gaze to find Marla standing with Shawn Foote. The two were huddled close as Shawn talked to her.

"Is something wrong?"

Jessica shook her head. "No, it's fine. It's just that Marla has a—"

He lost the tail end of her sentence. "What?"

She stood on tiptoe and cupped her mouth. "Marla has a huge crush on him. I'm proud of her."

"Ah. Good for her."

The song ended and another fast number took its place. "Is there somewhere quiet around here?"

"The only place I know of is the bathroom."

"No good."

"Oh," she said. "There's the roof."

"Perfect. Where's the door."

She pointed toward the kitchen. "At the back, to your left."

He laughed. "You're coming with me."

"No, I can't."

"You can." He grabbed her hand and led her through the press of bodies. It took a while, but they got past the dance floor. He'd even managed to snag a glass of champagne on the way.

The kitchen bustled with activity, but Dan didn't let her stop to investigate. He just kept leading her toward the door. When they reached the exit, Jessica put on the breaks. "Dan, I can't."

"Five minutes. We'll get some air, have a drink. Then we'll come on back and get as serious as you want."

"That's not the point," she said, clearly not ready to give in. But just then Owen McCabe saved the day. He was on the far side of the room, but he'd spotted them. His voice, calling out Jessica's name, was barely audible over the din.

"Uh-oh," Dan said. "Owen, six o'clock."

"Damn."

"Come on, before he gets any closer."

She let him pull her out the door, onto the metal steps leading to the roof.

They were in Midtown, on East Fifty-third between Lexington and Park, and when they'd climbed the two flights of stairs, they walked into a night filled with magic.

They weren't high enough up to have an unobstructed view, but what they did see was incredible. The Empire State Building and the Chrysler Building, lights blazing, made incredible exclamation points on either side. They were just high enough that the noise from the street was more of a whisper than a roar.

"There," he said. "Isn't this better?"

"Still, I should be—"

"You should be right here." He handed her the champagne. "Drink," he said. "Breathe. Relax. If nothing else, we need to make Owen wonder what we're doing."

She looked at the bubbly Dom Perignon, then back at him. "Okay. Five minutes."

"Is that all? Boy, you don't have very high expectations, do you?"

She seemed puzzled for a second, then she snorted in a very ladylike way. "You think Owen thinks we're out here having sex?"

"Well, yeah."

"Oh, that's just silly."

Now it was his turn to be skeptical. "You don't think that's the first thing he'd do if he had the chance?"

She paused. "Owen? Yes, you're probably right."

He stepped closer to her, touched her arm. "You don't think it's the first thing any man in that room would do if they had the chance?"

"Oh, please."

He pulled her close so he could feel her against him. "Do you have any idea how desirable you are?"

"Owen isn't here now."

"And for that, I'm truly grateful."

She finally met his gaze. He didn't hide his thoughts at all. And when he saw her touch her upper lip with the tip of her tongue, he bent down for the kiss that had beckoned all evening.

He wrapped her in his arms, not willing to chance her getting away, but from her response, the move was probably unnecessary. She opened her mouth just enough for him to fully taste her, to linger in that wet heat. She moaned, and he pressed against her, letting her feel what she did to him. Her little gasp told him he'd succeeded.

"I've wanted to do this since you walked out of the bedroom tonight," he whispered.

She responded with her lips, bringing him down again as she teased him with her tongue. His whole body tensed with the feel of her, with the electricity coursing through him. His hand moved slowly over the bare flesh of her back, the softness enough to drive him over the edge.

When he felt her fingers grappling at his back, he was the one to moan. He wallowed in her taste, moving his mouth to get her from every angle, to touch her completely and thoroughly, to possess her.

Pulling her tighter, closer, the party disappeared, the rest of Manhattan faded away, until all that existed were the two of them.

He rubbed against her, hard and anxious, letting her know that all she had to do was say the word—

"Jessica."

Owen's voice stopped them cold. She jerked back, pulling away as if she'd been burned.

"Hey there, Owen," Dan said, disliking the man more and more.

"Jessica," he said again, ignoring Dan. "I was looking everywhere for you."

"I was just taking a little break," she said. "Is there a problem?"

"*ET* wants an interview, and I thought you should get out there."

"I thought they wanted to talk to Sheree and Shawn."

"They do, but I think we need to have a presence."

"Okay, sure. I'll be right down."

Owen gave Dan a look that would singe the hair off his eyebrows. "I'll take you to them. They're not in the building."

She reached out and took Dan's hand. "Okay, let's go."

When Owen saw Dan was joining them, he wasn't pleased. The rest of the night was all business, but her thoughts never strayed too far from that kiss.

FIVE WORST GIFTS TO BUY A WOMAN

1. *Never give a woman any kind of household appliance or something that is going to make "housework" easier. For instance, a blender, a toaster, a new vacuum, anything in an infomercial.*

2. *Any sharp objects made by Ronco that slices or dices, or a set of Ginsu knives. These may one day be used as a weapon against you when you come home with lipstick on your collar after a "night out with the boys."*

3. *Any lingerie made of flannel. It gives her the idea that you do not consider her the sexy woman that she is. Take out that wallet and buy her something sexy from Victoria's Secret.*

4. *Any type of cubic zirconium jewelry you see on a home shopping channel.*

5. *Please do not buy her clothes because you think for one minute you have good taste in woman's clothing. Believe me, she'll smile and say it's beautiful, while choking back tears and mumbling under her breath, "Where the hell would I ever wear this outfit without being arrested for bad taste?"*

Source: JokesMagazine.Com "Ten Worst Gifts To Buy A Woman"
http://jokesmagazine.com/frontpage.asp

7

THEY LEFT THE PARTY at a quarter to three, the quiet of the limo startling after so much noise. Jessica seemed pleased and exhausted. From what he could see, the event had been every bit the success she'd been hoping for. It hadn't been as victorious for him, however.

The kiss on the rooftop haunted him. He'd felt something powerful up there, something that hadn't stirred in him for a long, long time.

Jessica leaned back on the black-leather seat and closed her eyes. His gaze lingered on her face, memorizing the lush curve of her lips. He wondered how much of what he felt was primal, and what part of it was his excitement at having someone with such an agile mind as a sparring partner.

The last woman he'd been involved with hadn't been nearly as bright as Jessica, although she was by no means dull. Lily had been an intoxicatingly beautiful woman and, had she tried, she could have done something with her life. She'd been preoccupied with her beauty, however, and spent inordinate amounts of time primping, shopping, anointing. In the beginning of the relationship, when it was filled with that first blush of excitement, he hadn't minded a bit. Eventually, though, he'd grown tired of it, preferring the company of his friends. She'd broken up with him, which had been a relief. That was over a year ago, during which time he'd had only one brief encounter, and that was with an old friend who'd visited from Oregon and had left after three wild days.

It wasn't a stretch to place his ardor for Jessica on the doorstep of lust. And yet, he was just as eager to talk with her as he was to make love to her. Well, maybe that was stretching it pretty thin. He definitely wanted to sleep with her, to explore all of her fantasies. In fact, that was something he intended to pursue as soon as he could. She'd sworn that she would tell the truth, and he was going to press her as far as he could. Get her to open up as no woman ever had, at least to him.

What did she fantasize about? It wasn't being tied up, that much he knew, but what? In her dreams, was she holding the reins? Or did she yearn for something sweetly romantic? God, he had to know.

She turned her head and opened her eyes just enough so she could see him. "Are we there yet?"

He looked out the window, recognizing the deli on the corner. "Soon."

"I don't think I have the energy to get out of the car."

He scooted over a bit, slid his arm in back of her so her head rested on his shoulder. "You can lean on me," he said.

She shifted a bit, getting comfy. "You were great tonight. Owen was only a minor nuisance."

"My pleasure."

"Sorry we didn't get that dance."

"I'm not worried about it. We'll have our chance."

She didn't say anything, and a few moments later her breathing was so slow and even, he thought she must be asleep. They'd be at the hotel in five minutes, so he'd have to wake her, but in the meantime, he enjoyed the feel of her resting against him. She was so warm, so delicate. His fingers brushed her shoulder, amazed at the softness, the creamy texture of her skin. Then his gaze moved down to her breasts, the tantalizing view a little too enticing.

It wasn't a wise thing to get all heated up, not tonight. She needed her sleep and he needed to get himself back on track.

The truth was, he didn't want to rush this thing. He wanted to complete his research, and do right by her. There was no rush. She wasn't going anywhere.

The limo turned the last corner and pulled in to the hotel. She woke when it came to a stop, sitting up with a little shake of her head. "We're here."

"That we are," he said, sorry that the ride had ended.

The door opened, and Dan got out, offering Jessica his hand. She took it and smiled as she got out. He tipped the driver, then put his arm around her shoulder as they made their way inside.

She didn't say anything on the ride up, and he felt just as comfortable in the silence. After a slow walk down the hall, they entered the suite. She stood quite still while he turned on some lights. When he walked back to her side, she reached out and grabbed his lapel, pulling him down to eye level. She kissed him softly on the lips, just a peck, really. "Thank you," she said.

He wanted more, but all he did was smile as she let him go. "You go ahead and use the bathroom first," he said. "You need to get to bed."

"I have to be up at seven," she said.

"Ouch."

"I'll say. But the only thing I have to do tomorrow is a photo shoot. Shouldn't be too bad."

"That sounds interesting."

"It won't be. But you can always watch the models change if you're bored."

"I'd never be that bored."

She gave him a half smile. "That's it. I'm falling asleep on my feet." She headed to her bedroom, weaving a little.

Dan watched her until she shut the door, then he reached up and undid his tie. He was glad the pullout bed was comfortable, because he needed his beauty rest, too. His jacket came off next, and then his cummerbund. Although he felt like tossing them all on a chair, and worrying about it in the morning, he hung them up like a good little guest. By then, Jessica had appeared in her kimono and hurried to the bathroom.

He stopped on his way to making his bed, staring at the bathroom door. Was she naked underneath that robe? He could picture her so clearly it was painful. He wanted to walk in on her, lift her up and sit her on the edge of the counter. Spread her legs apart and stand real close, so that the heat of her could warm his already hot body. Kiss her until she forgot about sleep, forgot about work. Run his hands over her stunning breasts, feel the heft of them, the rigid peaks of her nipples. He'd take his time tasting her, sucking each nipple until her fingers clawed his back.

And then he'd get on his knees, pulling her forward until her hot center was open before him. He'd work his tongue slowly, teasing all around her clit until she begged, and then he would be relentless. To make her come until she couldn't stand it another second. When she was almost to the point of madness, that's when he'd stand up. Hold her right there at the edge, and he'd enter her in one hard stroke, filling her, making her come yet again.

The bathroom door opened and he spun to his left, acutely aware of the bulge in his tuxedo pants. He didn't want her to think sex was all he ever thought about, although with her, that was mostly true.

"All yours," she said, and she made her way to the bedroom.

"Thanks," he said over his shoulder. He didn't relax until he was alone, and then, the relaxation only went as far as his shoulders.

He grabbed some pajama bottoms, which he didn't much care for. He slept in the nude, but his mother had gotten him the blue cotton pair two Christmases ago and he figured it was only right to put them on now.

Once in the bathroom, he turned on the shower, peeled off the rest of his clothes and stepped inside. He probably should have made the water cold, but that idea seemed excessive when there was a perfectly acceptable alternative.

He grabbed the soap and after a quick wash, he took matters into his own hands. Well, hand. Eyes closed, he thought about picking up where he'd left off, but he'd liked the foreplay too much. The venue changed to the living room. Right out there, with the couch already made into a bed. And Jessica wasn't in the kimono. No, she was wearing that incredible scarlet dress. He placed her in front of the sliding glass door. Behind it, Manhattan glittered like a jewel, but his gaze would be squarely on her reflection, so clear he could read her eyes as he stood close behind her. Close enough to nibble on the soft curve of her neck, right where it became shoulder. He'd run his fingers softly over the expanse of her back, giving her goose bumps, making her quiver. Then he'd find the soft little lobe of her ear and run his tongue up into the shell, then nip again at the lobe as he grasped her zipper and pulled it down, down.

His breathing got heavier as the images spilled in front of him, each more erotic than the next. But he didn't want it to end, not yet. There was still too much to see.

JESSICA SPREAD her legs, and ran her hand down her stomach as the images in her head went from hot to scalding. She'd tried to sleep, but it was useless. Not while Dan was on the other side of that door, and not with the memory of his kiss still on her lips.

My God, what he'd done to her. It was crazy. She hardly knew him, and she wasn't one of those fickle females who'd drop her panties at the first sight of a good-looking guy. Okay, so Dan was more than good-looking. He was incredible, and the way he kissed.

Her fingers found the fold of her sex, and she didn't waste any time going for the magic. She'd learned years ago to take care of her own needs, and saw nothing wrong with it. In fact, her ability to pleasure herself had kept her out of trouble on more than one occasion. Tonight, for the first time she could recall, she felt how incredibly lacking it was. Not that she couldn't get herself off, that was just a matter of imagination and persistence, but oh, how she wanted to feel him next to her. To see his body, to see what he would do with her.

His creativity, she felt certain, ran to more than just computer software. No, this was a man who would take his time. Who would use everything at his disposal to bring her pleasure. His kiss had told her so much…too much. And she wanted more.

She fixed an image in her head while she increased her speed and pressure. Dan, walking in right now, naked, hard. Big and hard. So hard. Throwing back the covers, catching her with her hand in the cookie jar. Giving her that wicked grin of his. Climbing onto the bed, pulling her hand away. Telling her to relax, and let him do the driving.

Her nipples hardened as she pictured him taking each one between his lips, circling, sucking, while his hands explored her body. She'd reach out and find that hard length of his and do her own exploration. There was something so intoxicating about the softness of the flesh encasing something so rigid. She loved playing with penises, although she didn't often get the chance.

But then she'd let him go as he slid down, licking her every inch of the way from her breastbone to her nether lips.

Oh, God, she had to slow down... If she didn't she would...

...COME. He wasn't ready yet, but dammit, the picture in his head! He had her up to the glass, so cold she'd cried out when her naked back had pressed against it. His hands holding her ass, holding her up so that her body was perfectly aligned for his entry. He'd taken her mouth with his, and kissed her deeply, and then he'd thrust inside her so hard he'd nearly lost it that second.

But he'd held on and now, in a picture so vivid he could practically taste her, he continued to thrust, pretending it wasn't his hand.

It was too late, he couldn't hold back another second. He pumped, fast, and his pelvis pushed involuntarily until there...there... "Jessica!"

"OH, GOD, Dan!" Jessica pulled her hand away and buried her head in her pillow. She'd been so loud, she'd probably wakened him, and that would be a disaster. She shivered as an after-thrill took her, then squeezed her legs tight as she tried to slow her breathing.

The door was thick, he probably hadn't heard. Or thought it was the TV. Or something. She couldn't worry about it, not when it was so late and she had to get up so early.

She fluffed her pillow, straightened the blankets and closed her eyes. And immediately pictured Dan. Naked.

This wasn't good. This wasn't good at all. She reached over and grabbed the remote, turning the TV onto a late-night black-and-white movie. She turned down the sound so it was just loud enough that she'd have to struggle to make out the words. That should do it. She hoped.

MARLA LOOKED at the clock on her bedside table. It was almost four, and she wasn't the least bit sleepy. She couldn't stop thinking about the night. About Shawn.

Oh, God, he'd talked to her so much! Every time he wasn't having his picture taken or doing some other work stuff, he'd come right back to her and just picked up the conversation as if it had never been interrupted.

It was simply too much. How she'd lived through it without doing something fatal was beyond her wildest imaginings. Shawn Foote. He'd laughed at her jokes, and most people didn't because her humor was, well, different, but he'd gotten her jokes, and it turned out his humor was also odd, and even though they were different odds, they still kind of matched, which was... Better than anything.

They'd talked about his work, and how he wasn't crazy about being a model, but they paid him so much money that he couldn't turn it down, but now that he'd invested a good portion of it, he was going back to school to study animal husbandry because what he really wanted was to have a big ranch in Montana with lots of horses and great fishing. And he wanted to have a whole bunch of cabins on his property so he could invite all his writer and artist friends to come and visit and stay as long as they wanted, which was the most wonderful thing she'd ever heard.

He'd asked all about her, too, and she'd told him about college and how cool it was to work with Jessica, and that she wasn't quite sure she wanted to stay in marketing, but she felt as if she had time to figure it out.

While she stood talking with him, a billion movie stars came to talk, and Shawn introduced her to each one as if *she* were the celebrity, which kind of made her nervous, but then it didn't because he was so relaxed about the whole thing. She'd met Drew Barrymore, Josh Hartnett, Hugh Grant, Gwyneth Paltrow and so many more, they blurred in her mind. All of them were so good-looking it made her feel lumpish, except Shawn was by far the best-looking guy there. She could tell that people were wondering what he was doing sticking by her all night, but she didn't care. Nothing could have been better than her night, not one thing.

Except perhaps the last few minutes, when Shawn had held her hand and had smiled that incredible smile that gave him dimples to die for, and this one lock of hair had been over his eye, and he'd said he had a really good time and he was glad the job wasn't over.

With the memory shimmering in her mind, she turned over, punched her pillow and started all over again from the beginning.

DATING TIPS FOR MEN

There are lots of ways to ruin a date. Here are a few things NOT to say on a date...

1. *I really don't like this restaurant that much, but I wanted to use this two-for-one coupon before it expired.*

2. *I used to come here all the time with my ex.*

3. *Would you excuse me? My cat gets lonely if he doesn't hear my voice on the answering machine every hour.*

4. *I really feel that I've grown in the past few years. Used to be I wouldn't have given someone like you a second look.*

Source: Thompson, Dave "Things Not to Say on Your Valentine's Date"
http://www.ijmc.com/

8

JESSICA WOKE to the annoyance of the alarm after what felt like ten minutes of sleep. She'd had a dreadful night, filled with sexual dreams, all of them starring Dan Crawford. Today was going to be relatively calm, and she felt sure he was going to start questioning her in earnest, which made her downright nervous. She was already too intimate with him, and answering him truthfully was going to be tricky. Maybe he wouldn't ask her anything that would betray her feelings toward him. Although, aside from wanting to sleep with him, she wasn't sure at all what those feelings were.

It shouldn't matter. She'd set her course and nothing was going to make her stray, not even a man as fascinating as Dan.

As she gathered her clothes, she thought about Carrie Elward, her roommate in college. Carrie had been a brilliant girl, top of her class. At graduation she'd already accepted a top-paying position at IBM, having had to choose among a host of equally enticing offers. That first year, she'd distinguished herself, saving the company several million dollars with a new program she'd developed, and her future seemed paved with gold. Then she'd met Alex, a stunning charmer from Canada who ran a small but successful dot-com. Within six months, Carrie had lost her luster, and at the end of the year she'd quit IBM to help Alex run his company. The bottom had fallen out shortly thereafter, and

Carrie had been reduced to taking a position at American Standard for half the pay.

It was a lesson Jessica took to heart. Not that it was fair. Men didn't seem to have the same difficulty mixing love and career. But no one had said life was fair. If she wanted to have the kind of security and power she dreamt of, there was no way she could get herself involved in a serious relationship. Later. All that was going to come, just not for a few years. Once she had a vice presidency, she'd be open to more, but until then, she'd be a fool to let her emotions ruin her future.

Maybe, if she was lucky, Dan would still be available, although that was a long shot. She was amazed he wasn't already married. But, he'd said he hadn't had much luck with women. She couldn't see it, unless he was sabotaging himself in some way. That was an all-too-common problem, easy to see in others, invisible to the one most affected.

It did feel weird helping a man she found so attractive gain the skills necessary to find another woman. But she'd promised, and she was a woman of her word.

She had all her things together and she left the safety of her bedroom to head for the shower. Her gaze went immediately to the table by the wet bar. Dan was dressed handsomely in a gray oxford shirt with casual jeans. Her blush spoke as much for her troubled sleep as it did for her immediate and powerful reaction to seeing him. The man was a walking pheromone.

"I hope you like it," he said.

She followed his gaze to the table, spread out with a large and abundant breakfast array. The plates were domed, so she couldn't tell what he'd ordered, but she could see orange juice, coffee, toast and a syrup container. "What's all this?"

"I figured we'd get a quiet meal in before we had to do the photo-shoot thing."

She headed toward the table, touched at his thoughtfulness. "It looks great."

"I wasn't sure what you liked, so I got some of everything."

She uncovered a plate of scrambled eggs, then another of pancakes. The scent reminded her of her hunger and she set her clothes on one of the chairs and sat in another. "This is very kind."

"No sweat." He sat opposite her and started to prepare his plate. Eggs Benedict, crisp bacon, hash browns. She took the scrambled eggs, sausage and the other half of the potatoes. For a while, they ate in silence, drank juice, prepared coffee. Then she noticed his silence, not of word but of gesture, and caught him looking at her with an expression she couldn't quite name. "What?"

"Nothing," he said, attacking his food again.

"Come on, I know you want to ask questions. It's okay. Ask."

He finished chewing, then stared at his fork for a minute. When he looked up, she found her tummy was tight.

"Why don't you want a relationship?"

She relaxed. This was an easy one. For the next few minutes she laid out the argument just as it had come to her such a short time ago. He didn't interrupt, just listened attentively, taking the occasional bite or sip. When she'd finished, she drank some coffee, debating the wisdom of having some pancakes.

"I know women with strong, successful careers who are married."

She knew it couldn't be that simple. "I'm sure there are, although I don't know any. The myth is that women can have it all. It's not true. Something has to give. I don't want to have to choose between my career and a man."

"I don't blame you. That would be tough. But I don't believe the choice would be difficult between a career and love. I think you can have both. In fact, I think that with someone there in your corner, someone who cares about you and what you do, the career would change into something much more meaningful. And, at the end of the day, you wouldn't be alone for your victories. Or your defeats."

"Being alone doesn't bother me. And, I might add, for a man your age, you certainly have an idealist view of relationships."

"Believe me, I've thought a lot about that. You're right. I am being idealistic. But I lived my whole life with two people who loved and respected each other. Watching them together made it impossible for me to settle for anything less."

She put down her cup. "I'm sorry for you."

His eyebrows rose in surprise. "Why?"

"Because what you saw with your parents is the exception to the rule. I don't know a single couple like that."

"I not only saw it with my parents, but several of their friends."

"You were lucky."

"So you think I should just give up? Settle for someone mediocre?"

"No. I don't think you should settle. Maybe adjust your expectations."

"To what? What are your expectations?"

"I'm not sure how to answer. I haven't thought about it that much."

"Seriously?"

"No. I've been pretty focused on what I've been doing."

"But surely you've thought about getting married. Having a family."

"Only in the vaguest terms."

"What was your family like?"

"Nothing like yours, that's for sure."

"Tell me."

She glanced at her watch. "I still have to shower and dress."

"We won't be late."

She supposed she owed him this, although it wasn't her idea of a good time. "My parents married young, after my mother got pregnant in high school. She ended up with her diploma, but only by the skin of her teeth. My father did two years of college, but never had the life he'd hoped for. He wanted to be a chemist, but he ended up settling for a job as a salesman for a pharmaceutical company. My mother had two more children, both girls, and then she and my dad divorced. My mother worked for years as a legal secretary, which she hated. Most of the people I grew up with came from similar backgrounds. No grand passionate love affairs that lasted past the seven-year itch."

"Wow. It makes sense that you've focused on your career."

"Yes, I suppose it does. But that doesn't mean I'm not happy."

"Are you?"

"Yes. I take a great deal of pride in my accomplishments. I've already got a nice portfolio started, and by the time I'm through, I expect to be very comfortable."

He leaned forward in his chair, which made her aware of her own body; leaning back, crossed arms, crossed legs. She made an effort to loosen up, but the best she could do was hold on to her cup of coffee.

"All on your own, right?" he asked.

"Exactly. I learned very early on that there isn't a knight in shining armor out there waiting to rescue me. If I want security, I'll have to earn it myself."

"That's wise."

"You agree?"

He spread his hands. "With the knight theory? Yeah, I do. I don't think it's good for anyone to wait to be rescued. It puts too much pressure on the rescuer. It can only lead to disappointment."

"But isn't that what you're hoping to do?"

"No, not at all. I expect the right woman for me will have found what makes her whole and happy. I want to share in that, just as I hope she'll share in my life."

"Don't you read? The statistics alone tell you that you're dreaming."

He frowned. "God, I hope not."

"I'm sorry. I don't mean to rain on your whatever. My experience has clearly been different than yours. You'll probably find just what you're looking for."

"I'm going to try," he said.

"Your parents, what do they think of this research project of yours?"

"My father died two years ago, but my mother thinks I'm nuts."

She smiled. "That's got to be hard about your dad. It sounds like you two were close."

"Oh, yeah. I'm sure he would have shared my mother's sentiments, but he would never have discouraged me. Mom, either. They believe in life by trial and error."

"So far, you seem to have done well."

He smiled. "No complaints. I'm about as happy as a man has a right to be."

"The statistics on that are pretty daunting, too."

He got a piece of bacon from his plate, ate it slowly. "I wonder why that is," he said. "So much angst. It never made sense to me."

"Speaking of angst, I'd better get my act in gear. We have to be at the shoot in less than an hour."

"Don't want any more breakfast?"

"Yes, but I'd better not. It was great. Thank you."

He smiled before he sipped some coffee. She gathered her things and headed for the shower, wondering if she had left because of the time or the conversation.

As soon as she was naked, her thoughts went to last night. The strength of her want of him. Breakfast had been terrific, but not filled with that same lust, although she still found him completely yummy. This was different. She'd never experienced this kind of balance before. Her past flings, and she knew that's all they were, had been like Roman candles. Brilliant flame, but short-lived. She'd felt that same intensity last night, but now the fire was banked, smoldering, while her focus had been on the conversation.

She climbed in the shower and began her regimen, all the while chewing on the situation.

DAN FOUND HIMSELF a director's chair and settled in for a long day. They had set up camp in a relatively quiet section of Grand Central Station, cordoned off from the public. The photographer was some big shot with a bunch of major campaigns under his belt, and the models were in the super category, including Sheree O'Brien and Shawn Foote.

It was interesting watching Marla around Shawn. She was clearly smitten, and he seemed interested right back. Surprisingly, Dan was worried for her. Even though he was staunchly in favor of tasting all that life had to offer, he liked Marla and didn't want to see her get hurt. Although he wasn't acquainted with Shawn, he had known some male models and actors, and those hadn't exactly been the brightest or the kindest people he'd ever met. Mostly, they'd been so obsessed with themselves, there was no room for anyone else in their lives. But, he'd give Shawn the benefit of the doubt. For now.

His gaze shifted to Jessica as she spoke with the photographer. Owen hovered, but so far he hadn't been a real pest. Jessica was in her glory, planning, arranging, making things happen. He liked watching her work. She wore her confidence like a comfortable sweater, and it made her even more beautiful. Today she had on pants, khaki colored, with a cream top and a matching jacket. The outfit would have looked plain on another woman, but it made her hair a more vivid auburn, and it complemented her skin.

He kept wanting to touch her. On the way down to the taxi he'd put his hand on the small of her back. She'd reacted with a little twitch, which was interesting, but her blush was more telling.

There was definitely something between them, the attraction wasn't one-sided. He saw a lot of the signs, the fidgeting with the hair, the sideways glances, those telltale blushes. Tonight, if they finished the shoot at a reasonable hour, they would have the evening free. He was going to take her to dinner, and he felt certain that he could steer the conversation into one of two directions. He could keep it intellectual, or he could just as easily swing it to the hot and heavy. Given free rein with the questions made either option viable. Of course, what he should do is stick to the plan. But the plan hadn't taken into account how much he wanted her.

''Do you mind?''

He looked up at the voice, startled. Standing close to his left was Sheree herself. She was dressed in a large, white, man's shirt with bicycle shorts peeking from the bottom. Her shoes were slip-ons, the better to change into whatever wardrobe they had planned for her.

Her hair was up in very large curlers, which didn't distract in the least from her astonishing good looks. Naturally, her makeup was heavy, but still, he could see the perfection of her face, the pure symmetry that was so prized. Her smile, however, suggested that her want of a seat wasn't just about available chairs. There was an invitation there, or at the very least a question.

He stood and held the back of the second director's chair. "Please, sit."

She did, and her smile broadened. "I'm Sheree."

"Dan Crawford."

"I saw you last night," she said. "But I didn't have a minute to come over and introduce myself."

"I'm sorry for that, but pleased you have some time today."

"God, I'll have gobs of time. I have four changes, and no one can decide where to start. It's always like this. They should just shut up and let the chick call the shots."

"You mean Jessica?"

"Yeah. At least she's got a plan. But everyone wants to be the boss."

"I suppose so."

"What's your role in all this?"

He nodded at Jessica, who had turned to watch him and his new friend. "I'm with the chick."

"Oh." Sheree studied Jessica for a long moment. "You two serious?"

"Yeah, pretty serious."

She turned back to him. "You fool around?"

He laughed. "Thank you, but no. I don't."

She shook her head, then lifted her hand to examine her nails. "Bummer."

He laughed again, but his attention was on Jessica. She wasn't looking happy. Just then, Owen came up behind her, and even from Dan's seat he could see the hand inching around her waist.

Jessica stepped back as Dan rose. He headed straight for the pair, making sure his smile wasn't forced. All he had to do was mark his territory, get Owen to back off. He was a little surprised at how his animosity toward this prick had grown. He didn't want him touching Jessica.

"Morning, Owen."

Owen's expression said it all. He wasn't pleased to see Dan. Not even amused. "Yeah. Morning."

Dan walked straight up to Jessica and said, "Honey, you've got a little something right on the corner of your mouth." Then he touched her there, rubbing nothing, but making sure Owen got the point.

He seemed to. The hand that had been on Jessica's waist was now at his side. His unsubtle scowl reminded Dan of a kid that lived in his building. Spoiled rotten, and not afraid to show it.

Dan leaned forward and gave Jessica a little kiss. Icing on the cake. This was supposed to be all for show, but the moment his lips touched hers, he forgot about Owen and everything else. It didn't last long, but the kiss had repercussions. His whole body reacted, came to attention. Not just the lower half, either. It was like touching a live wire.

Well, that answered his question about how to approach tonight. He was going to bring out the heavy artillery, the more intimate, the better.

Sex wouldn't ruin the project. It would just change it. He could deal with that.

QUOTES FROM WOMEN

1. *You see a lot of smart guys with dumb women, but you hardly ever see a smart woman with a dumb guy.*

   —Erica Jong

2. *I'm not offended by all the dumb-blonde jokes because I know I'm not dumb...and I also know that I'm not blond.*

   —Dolly Parton

3. *I've been on so many blind dates, I should get a free dog.*

   —Wendy Liebman

4. *In politics, if you want anything said, ask a man; if you want anything done, ask a woman.*

   —Margaret Thatcher

5. *I have yet to hear a man ask for advice on how to combine marriage and a career.*

   —Gloria Steinem

9

ONCE THEY WERE FINISHED with the shoot, Jessica let out a deep breath, and all her tension and stress with it. No work lay ahead of her until tomorrow afternoon, when she'd have to go to the Rainbow Room and make sure the party coordinator was moving apace. There would be a dessert-and-jazz evening starting at nine, with the guests being more of the celebrities, models and media. She stood under an archway just outside the terminal as Dan hailed a cab. As soon as one pulled up, he opened the door for her and she made her way through the ever-present crowd to climb in.

Once Dan was settled in next to her, he asked, "To the hotel first, or dinner?"

She hadn't thought much about eating, but now that he mentioned it, she found herself ravenous. "I'd like to change, get freshened up." She looked at her watch, and it was just past six. "Maybe we could find something at seven?"

"Sure thing." He told the driver where to take them, then he pulled out a cell phone and dialed a number. It was a while until he spoke. "Andy? It's Dan Crawford. Can you find a table for me and a friend at seven?" Nothing for a minute, then he smiled. "Great, see you then." He hung up, his grin looking mighty self-satisfied.

"Where?" she asked.

"You'll see."

"You're not going to make me dress up, are you?"

''Wouldn't dream of it.''

''Okay, then.'' She settled back for the ride home, twice as long with the heavy traffic.

Soon the sounds outside the cab window ran together and faded as her tiredness took over. She barely stirred as Dan closed the gap between them and snaked his arm around her shoulder. It seemed the most natural thing in the world to rest her head on his shoulder, to feel the warmth of his breath on her temple, the gentle brush of his fingers against her arm.

He'd been the perfect escort, everything she could have wanted for the job. Owen had been kept at something of a distance, although every chance he got, he cornered her and grilled her about her relationship with Dan. It had been almost too easy to answer his questions, and by the end of the day she figured she'd made significant headway. The only thing that had bothered her, aside from the attitude of the photographer, had been her reaction to the models. Not when they'd been working, but when they'd hovered around Dan. All of the women had, at one time or another, sat with him, talked with him, laughed at his jokes. It looked as if Dan had been enjoying himself immensely, which shouldn't have mattered a whit. But it did. She had found herself more than once walking over to him, touching him the way he touched her when Owen was near.

Dan was a free agent, and after this campaign was over she had nothing on him. He could date whomever he wished, and my God, those women were about as stunning as women get. Who could blame him for snapping up the bait. Each one seemed more eager than the last.

Finally, she'd asked Marla to go sit with him, even though the request was selfish, as Marla was all twittery about Shawn. He seemed like a good guy, and from what Jessica had heard of their conversations, he'd been really sweet when it came to Marla.

Jessica just hoped her assistant didn't get her hopes up. This was a job for Shawn, just as it was for Dan, and when it came to an end, they would both walk off into their normal lives with nary a thought about the two redheads.

She'd said as much to Marla, but it wasn't any use. The girl was smitten. Shawn was spectacularly good-looking, and any woman would have been flattered at the attention. But Marla was a little too sweet and innocent for her own good, and Jessica was sure she was going to pay.

But even that didn't seem so important, curled up in the comfort of Dan's arm. He smelled wonderful, clean, but with a hint of spice. His breath was sweetly cinnamon, and it made her think of the gentle kiss he'd given her earlier.

It hadn't been much of a kiss, nothing compared to the earthquake of last night, and yet she'd been thrilled by it, and for a long time after, her heart pattered fast in her chest.

Clearly, this attraction wasn't going away. In fact, each new day it grew deeper and more insistent. She felt quite sure, despite his protestations about his research, that something had to give, and give soon.

She sighed, and he hugged her to him. It felt as if she belonged there, as if she was safe. She tried to think if any man had made her feel like this, and came up blank.

Maybe it wouldn't be a bad thing to let nature take its course. Unlike Marla, she was a realist, and she knew that nothing was going to happen between them that would have a lasting impact. She wouldn't allow that. But at this stage of the game, not sleeping with him was probably going to cause her more stress and grief then just giving in.

So give in she would.

THE RESTAURANT was packed, with a long line out onto the street, just as Dan had anticipated. But Andy, the maître d', was an old friend, and had never made him wait. Once the cab dropped them off, he took Jessica's hand and escorted her past the line all the way to the dining-room entrance. There was Andy, looking damn fine in her black dress and fancy hairdo.

"Dan!"

"Hey, Andy." They kissed in the European tradition, with a little American hug thrown in for good measure.

"It's such a treat to see you," she said. "You have to try the salmon tonight. It's a new recipe, and it's heaven."

"Will do." He introduced Jessica, and then Andy led them to a quiet booth in a cozy corner. It was perfect.

After they were settled, and drinks had been ordered, Jessica turned to him. "Ex-girlfriend?"

"Who? Andy?" He shook his head. "Old friend. She used to be my ex-roommate's ladylove. They broke up a year ago, and I ended up getting closer to Andy than Gordo."

"So that's how you can get a reservation at Biggalow's? Last time I heard, you had to be at least an A-list star to get that kind of treatment."

"Just the luck of the draw. I don't have many connections in the city, and most of them are pretty obscure, but there are a few that have earned me major brownie points."

"Tonight, for example."

He just smiled. She looked so pretty in her pale green blouse and slacks. Like the restaurant, she wasn't fancy on the outside, but she had the real goods. She'd handled the day like a pro, and though he couldn't pass any tests on fashion photography, he thought it had gone well.

"Are you going to try the salmon?"

"If Andy recommends it, you can bet it's the best."

She closed her menu and leaned back on the soft leather seat. "Okay, then."

As if signaled, the waitress came to the table and wrote down their orders. All Dan wanted was to be left alone with Jessica. Now that he had his wish, he hesitated. Instead of just coming out with his questions, he drank his scotch and scanned the crowd. A lot of celebrities were in attendance, and he thought a few of them had been at the party last night. God, New York was a tiny place. Especially when it came to the places that were "in" like Biggalow's. Personally, his favorite restaurant was a little Italian joint three blocks from his place, and there was never a wait to get in.

"I'm surprised," Jessica said.

"About what?

"I figured you'd have asked me at least one embarrassing question by now."

"I'm going to. I'm trying to decide how deeply to embarrass you. I mean, we don't even have our salads yet."

"So it gets worse by the course?"

"Worse? I'm not trying to torture you."

She looked at him warily. "Right. Asking about my deepest, darkest secrets is just a pleasant way to pass the time."

"Well, it sure beats idle chitchat."

"I don't know about that. We could talk about the weather."

"Boring."

"Sports?"

"Unless I'm participating, I don't care for them."

"Not even baseball?"

"Yawn."

"Okay, how about the women in your life. That seems juicy."

"About as dull as golf, I'd say."

"I doubt it."

"You'd be wrong. But now that you bring it up, what about your love life?"

"What love life?"

"Nothing? Ever?"

"Passing phases, none noteworthy."

"Hard to believe."

"Intentional. You know—"

"Career above all."

"Damn straight.

"But that doesn't mean you've stopped having urges. Thoughts." He leaned over, moving close enough that he could almost touch her ear. "Fantasies."

"Ah, here we go."

"Damn straight."

She sighed as if it was all too mundane, but even in the dimmed lighting at their booth he could see the hint of pink on her cheeks.

"What," she asked, "do you want to know?"

"Let's start out with urges."

Her eyebrows rose. "Meaning?"

"Are they frequent? Do they come in cycles, like your period? Does something you see or someone you meet spark them?"

"Phew," she said. "Here I was worried you might get personal."

He grinned. "You have to admit, it's an intriguing way to get to know someone."

"I think I'll do some research of my own. Start asking you questions."

"Fire away. But only after you've answered me."

She sipped her drink, a whiskey sour, scanning the room all the while. Finally, just as he was going to nudge her, she faced him again. "The urges come and go, and I've never really thought much about what sparks them. They do seem to be cyclical, but some months are worse than others. And yes, sometimes I'll see a movie, or meet someone who will be the catalyst, but it's nothing that can't be controlled."

"What do you do about them?"

"Oh, God."

"Come on, Jessica. It's just biology."

"Dissecting a frog is biology. This is torment."

"Have another drink. Then give."

"All right, all right. I…" She cleared her throat. "I masturbate."

"Excellent."

"I didn't know I was going to be graded."

"You're not. It's just that I figured you'd be in charge in that area, as well."

"What do you mean?"

"You're a pretty together cookie, and you've made some tough choices. I couldn't imagine you not handling your sexuality in the same manner."

"Thank you. I think."

"Definite compliment."

"My libido thanks you, too."

Dan moved his leg so their thighs touched. She sat up straighter, but didn't shy away. Which meant he wasn't pressing too hard. Yet. "Do you use a vibrator?"

"Jesus, Dan."

"Don't start. You knew what you were getting into."

"Wrong. But okay. I'll answer, but only because I made a promise."

"Good. So, vibrator? Hand? Showerhead?"

"Yes, yes and sometimes."

He nodded, trying to give himself an air of a professional researcher and not a horny bastard who had a hard-on that could pound nails into plywood. "Any preference?"

"It all depends on the circumstances. When I just want to get off and get to sleep, I use BOB."

"Battery-Operated Boyfriend?"

She nodded.

"And when you want it to be more sensual? To last?"

"I pleasure by hand."

"Those are the ones I want to talk about."

"Of course."

He leaned closer, resting his elbows on the table. "I want to hear about those fantasies. The ones that keep you up for hours."

"I don't know, Dan. Yes, I promised to be frank, but I'm not sure I can be this frank. This is private stuff."

"That's the point."

"Still…"

Dinner salads and bread arrived, giving her a reprieve, but he wasn't about to let her off the hook. He could tell she was feeling more than discomfort, that the conversation, if played well, could lead to much pleasurable mischief. He intended to play it for all it was worth.

They ate for a bit, and he didn't push, but when she'd eaten her second piece of warm sourdough, and had just a few bits of arugula left in her bowl, he figured it was time. "You want another drink?"

"Yes," she said too quickly.

He ordered them both a refill, waited for the plates to be cleared, then turned just enough in his seat that she had his whole attention. "Shoot," he said.

"If only I could."

He laughed, but he didn't budge. "Tell me about the most frequent fantasy. The one you come back to the most often."

"I'm afraid you'll find it terribly pedestrian."

"Don't worry about it. Just tell me the truth."

"Fine. But if I burst into flames, you're explaining to the fire department."

"Deal."

He leaned back, making sure she couldn't see his crotch from where she sat. She didn't need to know what kind of reaction she was getting. At least not yet.

"I suppose the most frequent fantasy is the one where

I'm alone in a cabin in the woods. It's dark, and the winds are strong outside. I have a fire roaring in the fireplace.''

"What are you wearing?"

"A robe."

"The kimono?"

She looked at him as if he was getting close to some imaginary line. He leaned back an inch, put his hands by his sides.

"Sometimes. Sometimes it's another robe."

"Okay. Sorry to interrupt."

"It's your nickel."

"Right, but I'll try to be quiet."

"Okay, so where was I?"

"Alone. Cabin. Wind. Robe."

She frowned at her drink. "I'm warm, and grateful to be out of the cold. I lie down on a big fur rug in front of the fire, and I'm kind of mesmerized by the flames. Before I know it, I'm touching myself."

"How?"

She glared once, then went back to staring. "Slow, sensual. I'm in no rush. The crackling of the fire makes me drowsy, but not sleepy. My hand moves down until I find…''

He nodded.

"Then I close my eyes, and as it gets closer…"

He held his breath, praying she wouldn't stop.

"…I hear something. I open my eyes, and there's a man standing right next to me, watching me."

"Who is he?"

"I don't know. He's just a man. Dark, big, well-muscled. I don't know how long he's been there, and I'm not at all embarrassed at what he's seen. I just keep touching myself. He takes off his shirt, then his boots. And then he reaches for his belt.

Dan had to have a drink. He wanted to place the glass

of ice on his erection, but he thought that might be a little blatant.

"He undoes his fly, and slowly takes off his pants. He's, uh, hard."

Dan coughed.

She glared again.

"Sorry."

"This is hard enough."

"I'll say."

That got him another glare. But it didn't stop her. She just found that fascinating glass again, and went on. "Once he's undressed, he lies down next to me. We kiss. For a long while. Then he starts touching me in the same places I touched myself. First, my breasts, but it's different because his hands are so large and rough. It's a totally different experience. He tells me to stop. To touch him instead, and I do. Then his hands move down my body until he, you know."

"Yeah."

"And he starts rubbing in small circles, the pressure is just right, not too hard or soft, and he keeps rubbing, and I let him go and I start getting closer and closer, and then I come like gangbusters, howling, and he climbs on top of me, spreads my thighs with his legs and he slams into me like he's found the mother lode."

Dan exhaled a breath he'd held forever. Jessica slugged back the rest of her drink. The waitress coughed, put their drinks down and backed away, her face as red as the cherry in her whiskey sour.

FIVE FACTS YOU SHOULD KNOW ABOUT MEN

1. *Men like to barbecue. Men will cook if danger is involved.*

2. *Men who have pierced ears are better prepared for marriage. They've experienced pain and bought jewelry.*

3. *Marrying a divorced man is ecologically responsible. In a world where there are more women than men, it pays to recycle.*

4. *All men hate to hear "We need to talk about our relationship." These seven words strike fear in the heart of even the strongest male.*

5. *Men have higher body temperatures than women. If your heating goes out in winter, sleep next to a man. Men are like portable heaters that snore.*

Source: Hope, Paco "Facts About Men"
http://funnies.paco.to/factsOnMen.html

10

_____

MARLA LOOKED in the bathroom mirror and held back a grin. About ten minutes ago, she'd covered her face with a bright green herbal mask, one she'd found in *Cosmo,* that was purported to make her skin positively glow. She'd also conditioned her hair with mashed bananas, and timed it so that she could wash the whole mess off at once. But that wasn't for another fifteen minutes. In the meantime, she'd pulled out her razor and shaving cream and sat herself on the bathroom counter to start the long and tedious process of removing all signs of hair from the neck down.

Of course, her thoughts were on the day, on the incredible time she'd spent with Shawn. Yeah, yeah, she knew it didn't mean anything, but he'd been so extraordinarily nice to her, it seemed like a dream.

They'd talked about his childhood and hers, which weren't so terribly different. She'd been the youngest of four, he of five. She'd gotten a strange sort of encouragement from her parents to stretch herself and accomplish, where he'd had the faith of his mother to buoy his spirits. Where they differed most was that Shawn's father was a dour and uncompromising man who had believed Shawn's looks automatically made him suspect, and he'd tormented his son constantly, accusing him of being a "fag" and of having feminine ways. His father's treatment had been terribly hard on Shawn, who was a sensitive boy, and had caused him to be wary of every emotion.

Finally, in college, at the University of New Mexico,

Shawn had had a revelation: he wasn't gay, wouldn't turn gay, and whatever anyone else thought of the situation was their own problem. From then on, it was easy to accept the modeling jobs that had been offered. He'd left school with two years to go when the offer of riches became too great to ignore.

He'd moved to New York four years ago and had met with success he could never have imagined. He'd been in countless magazines, on television, on billboards, including one so famous it had become something of a risqué icon. It was simply him in a pair of boxer shorts, and people from as far away as China recognized him instantly. Fame had its drawbacks, however, most of which centered around lack of privacy, but he'd said he figured there was always a price to pay for the kind of life he was living, and he'd grown accustomed to it.

He'd gone back to school against the advice of his agent and manager, but he didn't lose any sleep over it. He had a plan, and it promised him a wonderful future.

Marla had told him of her college days, and how she never truly fit in with any crowd she'd found. She wasn't as silly as the beer-drinking kegger lovers, and not so serious as the math geeks, but somewhere in between. She'd had a few good friends, but mostly she stuck to studying and listening to music. After she graduated, she'd researched the market carefully and had been offered four excellent jobs, but it was Jessica she wanted to work with. She'd never regretted the choice, although she didn't see herself following Jessica's strict "work-only" ethic. Marla still loved music, mostly classical and oldies, with some musicals, particularly those of Stephen Sondheim, to round out her tastes. That's when Shawn had smiled that unbelievable smile at her. "I know him," he'd said.

"Stephen Sondheim?"

"Yes. He's a friend. I could introduce you."

She'd been dizzy with the joy of it. To meet Stephen Sondheim would thrill her to her toes, but to have Shawn introduce him! It was simply over the top.

She finished shaving the one leg and picked up the canister to get the other one creamy, when the phone rang. Marla climbed down from the counter and hurried to the other room, a combination living room, kitchen and bedroom, to get the phone, fully expecting the call to be from Jessica.

It was Shawn. His sweet low voice took her breath away, and she didn't say anything for a minute after his hello. He repeated the word, and she remembered how to talk. "Hi."

"Am I bothering you?"

"Oh, no. No bothering here. In fact, the opposite of bothering which would be, uh… I don't know what the opposite would be but you're doing it. Nope. No bothering."

He laughed, which made her all smiley and giddy. She sat down on the edge of the couch, crossed her clean-shaven leg over the hairy one.

"What are you up to tomorrow?" he asked.

"We have the dessert-and-jazz party at the Rainbow Room."

"That's tomorrow night."

"I know, but I'll have to go there in the afternoon to make sure all the decorations are up and stuff like that."

"Ah, what time would that happen?"

"I'm not a hundred percent sure, but probably around two."

"Which would mean you would be available if, say, someone wanted to take you to brunch?"

That feeling swamped her tummy again, the one where the butterflies all took off at once and did the waltz. "Brunch?"

"You know, the meal that's not quite breakfast and not quite lunch."

"Yeah, I know. I've had brunch before. Once when I was eleven, we stayed in Las Vegas and we had brunch every day for a week. I ended up overdosing on pancakes and cheesecake."

"So, is that a yes?"

"Yes!"

"Good. How about I pick you up at ten?"

"Pick me up? You don't have to do that. I'm not at the hotel. I'm at home because I had things to do, and I'm sharing the room there with this other girl, you met her, Vicky, she's got brown hair and wears tights all the time, and anyway, she has all this stuff in the bathroom, which is fine, really, but hard to get around, so I decided to come home tonight to do all my girlie stuff…" She sighed. "Too much information, huh?"

"No, not at all. However, I did know you went home."

"You did?"

"I called you, remember?"

"Oh. Yeah. How?"

"On the contact sheet from the agency."

"Oh."

"So I'll pick you up, if, that is, you tell me where."

"Oh, okay." She gave him her address, and midway between her explaining where it was, he interrupted to tell her he already knew.

She closed her mouth, afraid it would start babbling on its own if she opened it even a bit. But then, he said, "See you at ten," and she said, "Okay," and then he hung up. She leaned her head on the phone for a second, wondering what she'd done in a previous life that could give her this in the present one. Whatever it was, she was grateful for it.

When she replaced the phone on the hook, it was mushed with lots of green gook from her face. After cleaning the receiver, she rushed back to the bathroom to finish shaving so she could take a shower. It was well past the time she should have washed off, so her face would be extra glowy. Which was nice, because then it would match how she felt.

JESSICA DIDN'T SAY anything for a long time after the waitress made her getaway. She was embarrassed, sure, but not terminally. She just wasn't certain what to say next. How does one follow that?

Finally, she looked over to see Dan, who was laughing. His face was kind of scrunched up, but on him it looked good. She smiled, appreciating the joke, but also a little concerned. The telling had taken a toll. The erotic frisson had dissipated somewhat, but there was a lingering sensation in her lower parts that made her shift on her seat. He stirred her up, this man. Something fierce.

Yes, she'd decided to go with the flow, so to speak, and scratch her proverbial itch. But something else nagged at her, and it was a little voice in the back of her head that said this wasn't all about sex. And if it wasn't just about sex, then having sex might not be the right way to go. Having sex might lead to wanting more, and more was what she shouldn't have.

All she had to do was think about the end of the campaign and the potential jobs that waited for her. On the other hand, the distraction of the attraction was quickly becoming too much to ignore, and that could easily lead to disaster.

"Now, that was a moment I won't soon forget," Dan said, wiping the corner of his eyes with his napkin. "The look on her face. Five'll get you ten, we have another waitress serving us the rest of our meal."

"I won't take that bet." She sipped her new drink, careful not to down too much, as she was hungry as a hound and the liquor would hit too hard. "I think they're probably all pulling lots to see who has to serve us."

"You certainly took it all with a grain of salt."

She shrugged. "Not much I could do about it once it was done. Why fret?"

"Why, indeed?" He held up his glass. "To stoicism."

She clicked her glass to his and took another sip. "I hope they don't haggle too much. I'm starved."

"Me, too."

They both turned toward the kitchen, but no waitress appeared, so they settled back to wait.

"That was great, by the way," he said. "Just the kind of thing I was looking for."

"But aren't there a whole bunch of books that detail women's sexual fantasies? Couldn't you just read them?"

"I did, and they didn't work. Anecdotal evidence from a cross section of anonymous women is fine, but it doesn't get to the heart of what I'm looking for. I'm thinking that if I can understand one particular woman, you, then I'll see all women in a new light."

She shook her head. "Hasn't every man since Adam tried to figure us out, and failed?"

"Exactly what makes the research so interesting."

"You know what I think?"

"What?"

"I think you're a closet voyeur, and you're getting your jollies asking me all this embarrassing stuff."

Instead of the laugh she expected, his eyebrows furrowed and he frowned. "It's possible that's true, although I haven't sought out voyeuristic situations in the past."

"I was kidding."

"I know. But I don't think it's something I can simply dismiss out of hand."

"What?"

"I have to be honest with you, Jessica. I'm not the model of stoicism you are. When you were recounting your fantasy, it wasn't all science and note-taking here."

"It wasn't?"

He shook his head. "No. There was a decided uprising, if you get my drift."

She hid her smile behind her whiskey sour. "Oh, dear."

"Yeah."

"Well, maybe we should call it off? The research, I mean."

He hesitated, but not for long. "No, I don't think so. I think we should press on."

"But what if there's another 'uprising'?"

He scooted a little closer to her. "It's a very real possibility."

"Oh?"

He nodded, moved closer still. "However," he said, keeping his voice low, unreachable to any nearby waitress, "I believe that my reaction is an important factor in the project."

"How so?"

"If I wasn't turned on, then you wouldn't be the right subject."

"Hmm. So it's not any particular woman. It's a particular woman you're attracted to."

"Exactly. And it's equally important that the woman— you—be attracted to me."

She frowned. "Oh, dear."

The look on his face was priceless. Total shock. She hadn't thought of him as egocentric, and he certainly hadn't behaved like one of those guys who think they're God's gift, but it was clear he'd sensed the heat between them. She decided to be kind, and let him off the hook. "Kidding," she said. "I'd be lying if I said it wasn't so."

He relaxed visibly. And touched the back of her neck with his fingers. Her reaction was instant and intense. Heat, moisture, rapid breathing, a flush to her cheeks.

He evidently saw the signs, and probably suspected the

rest. But just then their food arrived, via a waiter this time, and they both dug in like starving sailors.

After the initial emergency was over, and they could stop to savor the delicious meal, Dan touched her thigh. "You don't have to do anything else tonight, right?"

She shook her head.

"Great."

"Why?"

"I'm not close to being finished with my questions."

"I do have to get a good night's sleep."

"You'll sleep."

"Promise?"

"You bet. My job is to help you with your campaign, not hurt it."

"True."

They ate again, the rest of the night swimming with possibilities, stirring the air between them. When Jessica hit bottom and pushed away her plate, he dropped his fork and called for the bill. The waiter asked if they wanted dessert, and they said an abrupt "No!" at the same time.

"Not that I'm anxious," he said.

"Of course not," she agreed.

But he paid in record time, leaving a generous tip, while she hailed a taxi.

They didn't say a word as they headed toward the hotel. Not one. But she heard him. His intentions, his curiosity, his desire. She felt him, too, although all he touched was her shoulder, briefly.

By the time they reached the Willows, she was at the end of her rope. The elevator took forever, he fumbled with the key, and then finally, thank God, they were inside, the door was locked, and they were in each other's arms before she could say, "Take me, you fool."

Dan pulled her tight against him as he moved her toward the bedroom. Everything in his body cried out for being naked. Now. But he didn't know how Jessica would react to making love on the carpet, so he focused the one tiny section of his brain that wasn't completely fogged over with sex and manfully pressed on. She stumbled over something, and he realized it would have been a good thing to have turned on the light, but he wasn't about to let go, or God forbid, stop kissing her, not when her tongue was so busy exploring every inch of his mouth, and certainly not when he'd already managed to unbutton half her blouse, but then he almost tripped over the coffee table, and he said, "The hell with this," and he lifted her into his arms as if he was Tarzan or something, and not giving a damn what he tripped over, he made it to the bedroom and more importantly, to the bed.

Once he had her safely down, he reached to the side table and turned on the light. He wanted to see her. All of her. Every step of this glorious dance.

She lay panting, her blouse half-open to reveal a peach lace bra that couldn't hide her very erect nipples. The sight spurred him into action, and he ripped at his own shirt.

That got Jessica moving, too, and they raced to shed their clothes as if they were on fire. Which, in fact, they were.

By the time he got completely undressed, she'd reached the last stage—her panties. He held out a hand. "Stop."

She obeyed, her gaze moving down his chest, his stomach, finally his erection. He'd never been harder, of course she couldn't know that. But from the look on her face she wasn't displeased.

"Why am I stopping?" she asked, her gaze never moving up, even an inch.

"Because if we keep going at this pace, it's going to be a very wonderful yet very short experience."

"Short, my ass."

He laughed. "Thank you, but not what I meant."

"Oh. Right."

"So let me just appreciate you for a minute."

"Appreciate, how?"

"Looking," he said, climbing onto the big white bed. "And touching," he said, while his hand went to cup the most beautiful breasts he'd ever seen. When his hand came to rest on the perfect bosom, he nearly came, which would have been oh-so-unfortunate. The clever thing to do would be to think about baseball scores or perhaps mealworms. But he couldn't. All he could think about was how stunning she was, and how lucky he was, and how to be inside her was perhaps the most important thing in his whole life. He wanted it to last forever. He knew that couldn't be so.

"Dan?"

"Yes?"

"May I make a suggestion?"

"If it's about stopping this, no."

"On the contrary," she said, moving her lips very close to his. "I was thinking that we don't have to do this only the one time."

"Good, good."

She sighed into his mouth, making his cock twitch. "You're not getting it. First time fast. Second time slow."

He blinked, leaned forward and kissed her hard. "Jessica, you're a genius."

"Yes, I know."

MORE FACTS YOU SHOULD KNOW ABOUT MEN

1. When four or more men get together, they talk about sports.

2. When four or more women get together, they talk about men.

3. If a man says, "I'll call you," and he doesn't, he didn't forget...he didn't lose your number...he didn't die. He just didn't want to call you.

4. Getting rid of a man without hurting his masculinity is a problem. "Get out" and "I never want to see you again" might sound like a challenge. If you want to get rid of a man, try saying, "I love you...I want to marry you...I want to have your children." Sometimes they leave skid marks.

5. Men forget everything; women remember everything. That's why men need instant replays in sports. They've already forgotten what happened.

Source: Hope, Paco "Facts About Men"
http://funnies.paco.to/factsOnMen.html

11

PLEASED WITH HERSELF, and even more pleased with the man on top of her, Jessica smiled slowly, watching him watching her. He clearly liked what he saw, finding wonder in whatever his gaze caught, as if each square inch held new delightful surprises. It made her feel beautiful and desirable and it stirred the pit of her stomach, no, lower.

She ran her hand down the length of his arm from shoulder to wrist, softly caressing, pleased with the suggestion of corded muscle and the silky softness of hair. When she paused, she tried to circle his wrist with her thumb and index finger, but she couldn't. She stared at him all the while, noticing a tiny twitch of his right eye, the way his nostrils flared, and his white teeth, not perfectly even, but made endearing by slight imperfections. It was as if her vision had gone far beyond the traditional twenty-twenty into a new kind of sight. Not just because they were so close to one another, but because a veil of ordinariness had been lifted. She could read him like a book, his need, his tension, his excitement and his pleasure. More than simply observing, she was empathically connected to him, feeling the very things she witnessed on his face. She wanted him inside her, to make the connection stronger still. Something way beyond the five senses was at work here, and the closer they become the stronger it would become.

She shifted beneath him, him so still and watchful, and she lifted his large wrist, moving his hand to the lower regions of her stomach. His eyes widened, dilated so that there was only a thin circle of hazel left.

He leaned forward, near enough that their breath mingled, but she didn't close her eyes. Enraptured by his face, his scent, she met his gaze only inches away from her own. She expected a kiss, but instead, he licked her lower lip with his tongue, like a mother cat to her kitten. His hand inched downward, underneath her panties, until she felt him in her thatch of curls, and then, his fingers touched the upper folds.

He moaned very deep in his throat, using his talented tongue to taste her upper lip as he dipped inside her.

She closed her eyes, not because she wanted to but because the sensations were too strong. Her poor little brain couldn't process so many stimuli at once, so feeling won out over sight.

Her legs parted farther and he explored the soft, wet flesh between, inching down with the pads of his fingers, gently stroking as if she was skittish and he needed to calm her.

She didn't want to be calmed. When he plunged inside her using two fingers, she moved those last inches that separated their mouths, kissing him hard, sucking his tongue as if it would save her.

He moaned again, and she felt the vibration in her lips, her chest. She bucked against him, forcing his fingers deeper.

He pulled back, both finger and tongue, leaving her, she prayed not for long.

He got to his knees, straddling her. She wriggled a bit and got a smile in response.

A tearing sound distracted her and she looked down to see him pull a rolled condom out of a silver packet. She watched, engrossed, as he unrolled it over his thick flesh. Then his hands moved to her hips where he grasped her panties and pulled them slowly down.

He ran into a snag where his legs and hers touched. Instead of moving, he grasped one edge of her bikini panties in both hands and tore them apart. The sound, the rip, louder than their breaths combined. He looked exceedingly pleased with himself as he dropped the ruined material. Patiently, slowly, he lifted one knee and moved it inside the V of her legs. Then he moved the other until she bracketed him. But it was clear his hold was superior as he pushed her knees apart, wider and wider until he was satisfied. His gaze wandered down from her face to her chest to the view he'd just created. His breath quickened, his chest expanding and contracting like a runner's, his lips parted, his hands fisted at his sides, then opened with effort.

She felt exposed, more naked than naked as he looked at her with his raw hunger, and she wanted him to enter her, to take her now.

Just as she opened her mouth to beg, he leaned down and braced himself with corded arms on either side of her. He shifted his weight to the left as he used his right hand for guidance.

As she felt the tip of him touch her lips, he whispered, "Jess," forcing her gaze to meet his.

The connection was electric and wondrous as he slid into her wet folds inch by slow inch, filling her with his body, becoming something greater than him and her.

Both arms now flexed on either side of her as he balanced on hands and knees. The tension in his body was like a bowstring, bunching tighter and tighter, even the cords in his neck. He stared at her, his intensity making her tremble as he thrust in, pulled out, thrust in again. She grasped the comforter in both fists, pulling the material up from the bed. Her hips rose to meet his challenge, and they found a feral rhythm that linked bodies and heartbeats.

There were no words for the feel of him inside her, only grunts and moans, primal and exotic.

Dan's eyes closed as his thrusts quickened, and her body responded in kind. It was coming, the coil of tension deep in her body like a spring pulled taut. Her mouth opened and she heard her own high keen as if from someone else, someone far away, and then the sound changed and it was her again, as the last bit of tension snapped with an orgasm that started between her legs and spread like a raging fire throughout her body.

He grimaced, arching his neck, his head thrown back with a roar. One final thrust, so fierce she was pushed up the bed, and then he froze, straining, and she trembled as another wave of pleasure burst inside her.

The room darkened around her, her vision narrowing to the circle of his face, still strained to the edges of endurance, his lips curled back, his chin jutting out, his Adam's apple too large in his throat.

A moment passed, another spasm racked her, and then she felt her hands and her hips, felt the air in her lungs, heard him take a ragged breath as he relaxed.

He looked down and gave her a slow smile. "Holy shit."

"I concur," she said, surprised her voice sounded so normal.

"So it wasn't just me?"

She shook her head. "Nope."

His smile broadened. "Cool."

Raising her hand, she brushed back his hair from his forehead, enjoying the silky texture between her fingers. "Does that blow your whole project?"

"Project? Oh, yeah. No. Not at all. I'm thinking it's a good thing."

"Oh?"

"Uh-huh." His smile faded. "I don't want to but I have to."

"What?"

"Move."

"Ah."

He slipped out of her and rolled to her side. For a moment, her gaze rested on the rise and fall of his chest, then she looked up. "How is it a good thing?"

"For one thing, I can maybe think a little more clearly."

"How so?"

"Wanting you was kinda filling up all the synapses."

"I see."

"And also, I'm thinking we've shared something pretty damn intimate, so that it'll be easier for you to answer my questions."

"Maybe. Maybe not."

"You don't think this was intimate?"

She gave him her "Well, duh" look. "I'm not sure what this new level of intimacy will do. What if I'm shier?"

Having quieted his breathing, he rolled over on his side, holding his head up with one hand. "Let's test it. What's the most wicked fantasy you've ever had?"

"I thought we'd covered fantasies."

"Nope. Barely scratched the surface."

"Oh."

"Come on. I'm looking for the filthiest, most disgusting thoughts you've ever had. The one that would get you arrested in every state but California."

She laughed. "Like I'd tell you."

His mouth widened in mock dismay. "You promised! You gave me your word."

"Some things are better left a mystery."

"No way. Uh-uh. I can't believe you're wimping out on me like this. I thought I knew you, but clearly, I was sadly mistaken." He let his head drop to the arc of his elbow. "After I've given you the best days of my life."

"Oh, please."

"No, no. Don't try to make it up to me. The tie between

us has been broken irrevocably." He put his fist on his chest. "I'm wounded to the core."

"All right, tell you what. You tell me your most disgusting fantasy, and then I'll tell you mine."

His head was up in a second, resting once again on his hand. "Really?"

"You are nothing but a scoundrel, that's all."

"True, but an earnest one."

She narrowed her eyes. "Answer me this. Even if you do tell me something vile and disgraceful, how will I know it's the worst you've got? Maybe you have a whole trove of disgusting things, and you're telling me some old run-of-the-mill horrifying perversion."

"Have I ever lied to you?"

"I have no idea."

"The answer is no. I have never. And I will never."

"So you say."

"Maybe this is just your way of chickening out?"

"Maybe it is."

"No fair."

"Ah, Danny boy, I hate to have to tell you, but no one said life was fair."

He got that shocked look again. "What? Say it ain't so."

"So."

"I hate that."

"Me, too."

He looked at her for a long minute. "You know what? We're going to have to postpone this chitchat for a minute. You wait right there. Don't go anywhere."

She crossed her heart. "Promise."

He climbed off the bed and headed for the bathroom while she shamelessly stared at his cute butt. When he was out of range, she let her head fall back on the pillow and closed her eyes.

It was without doubt the best sex she'd ever had. By a lot. There had been moments... Incredible. But also scary.

When he'd pulled away, she'd felt as if she'd lost some part of herself. Surely that wasn't normal for casual sex. Always before, even with men she'd really liked, there had been a slight feeling of relief when it was over. She'd never been the cuddling kind, and had been accused of being like a guy when it came to this sort of thing. That's why she didn't bring men home. Because she needed to make a quick getaway. But with Dan, all she'd wanted was to stay close. She wouldn't have objected to a cuddle here and there. Weird. Dangerous.

Her gaze moved to the door. The most worrying thing about him wasn't this, although it came close, but the fact that try as she might, she couldn't find anything wrong with him. No one was perfect. No one she'd ever met was near perfect. So what was his flaw? Did he hide behind his research? Was he commitment phobic? Did his relationships really end because they weren't meant to be, or did he change when he fell in love?

It was something to think about. Not that it mattered all that much, because there was no way in hell she was going to get involved with him, but still. It was a puzzle. Perhaps, if it were another time in her life, she'd want to get to the bottom of it. As it was, she'd better keep a clear head. Sex was sex. Even great sex. Not one thing more.

She sat up, looked at the torn Victoria's Secret panties bunched around one leg. Pulling them free, she tossed them into the wastebasket as she went to the closet and got her robe. It was late. She'd better get to sleep. Tomorrow was going to be a busy day.

DAN RAN HIS HAND through his hair, anxious to get back to Jessica, whether it was for talk or something more personal, although the discussion so far had certainly piqued his interest. He couldn't get over what had just happened. Jesus, it was the most intense encounter he could ever remember. Maybe it was the extended days of foreplay, but he doubted it. Something was happening between them, although he wasn't about to try to define it. What was needed here was further investigation. Some hands-on research. His favorite kind. He hadn't lied when he said this was a good thing. With Jessica, the exploration into her psyche, her sexuality, her modus operandi, would certainly be illuminating. Revelatory. Fascinating. He couldn't wait to dig in, and not simply with questions about her fantasy life, but her motivations, her perspective on the male of the species, the why and wherefore of her very being.

To know someone that well would, he felt sure, be life-changing. He'd known some women pretty well, Tamara and Kathleen to be sure, and yet neither of them had spurred this level of interest. By some wild fluke of fate, he'd been given access to someone who not only stirred him intellectually, but emotionally and physically as well. It was like discovering Tutankhamen, a perfect, untouched cache of incalculable worth, ready to be examined piece by piece, treasure by treasure.

He crossed the dark living room, his pace quickening as he neared the bedroom. Only, when he got to the door, he saw the empty bed. A flash of blue caught his eye and he turned to find Jessica standing by the closet, her kimono belted tightly at her waist, her arms crossed over her chest. The vibrant open woman he'd left on the bed had disappeared, replaced by someone he didn't know. Closed, reticent, distant. What in hell had happened in those few minutes he'd been away?

She smiled, but there was no pleasure in her eyes, only wariness.

"What's going on?"

"I saw what time it was. I'm not going to have many

nights where I can get a good night's sleep, so I'd better take advantage of it.''

Even her voice sounded unfamiliar. He felt naked and vulnerable standing in front of her, so he went to the pile of his clothes he'd so mindlessly tossed at the edge of the bed. He pulled on his pants before he turned to her, using the time to put together his thoughts, pushing his anger back so he could try to understand this strange twist.

When he faced her again, it dawned on him that she'd felt the same astonishment he had, and this was her way of dealing with it. Of course.

"What's that look?" she asked.

"Nothing. I'm thinking you're right. That you should get your rest."

Her shoulders relaxed. "Not that I didn't enjoy—"

"I know. Me, too. You're amazing. But the priority is the campaign, and I'm here to help. So why don't you go do whatever voodoo you do in the bathroom, and we'll call it a night."

"Oh, okay." Her smile wavered, and for a moment he thought she was back, but then she straightened, avoided his gaze. "Thanks."

"No sweat."

She walked past him, not too closely. And then she was gone.

More disappointed than he cared to admit, he got his shirt, shoes, socks and headed for the living room. His gaze moved to the closed bathroom door. He tossed his clothes to the floor beside the couch and threw the pillows on top of them. He yanked the bed out so roughly the whole couch moved, but he didn't give a damn.

Okay, he'd let her off the hook. She was scared. He got it. His mother would be proud. So why was he so pissed off?

He'd been cheated. Even though he saw the reason, saw

the fear in Jessica's body language, it didn't matter. He'd been happier than he could remember just ten minutes ago, excited as a kid with a brand-new bike.

Which had just been taken away.

He got undressed again, waited a moment to see if she would come out of the bathroom, and maybe... But the clock kept ticking, and soon he wasn't particularly interested in whether she came out or not.

He crawled under the sheets and beat his pillow into submission. He heard the bathroom door open, saw the light behind his eyelids dim as she flipped the switch, heard the soft footpads as she crossed the carpet to her bedroom. Even though she tried to keep it quiet, he could hear the click of her door as she shut him out.

Sleep didn't come for a long, long time.

DIFFERENCES

In arguments a woman has the last word. Anything a man says after that is the beginning of a new argument.

A woman worries about the future until she gets a husband. A husband doesn't worry about the future until he gets a wife.

A woman will dress up to go shopping, water the plants, empty the garbage, answer the phone and read a book. A man will get dressed up for weddings and funerals.

Source: Orton, Joe ''Men and Women Compared''
http://www.orton.demon.co.uk/ff/

12

JESSICA STARED at the ceiling, more precisely at the dark area above her bed. For all her protests that she needed a good night's sleep, she certainly wasn't getting one. The last time she'd looked at the clock, it had been two-fifteen. She kept closing her eyes, doing relaxation exercises, but her thoughts kept returning to Dan and how she'd left things.

She could tell he was angry. Not that she blamed him. Talk about doing a one-eighty. The poor guy hadn't had a lick of warning. On the other hand, it was probably best that she'd nipped their little boink-fest in the bud. It didn't feel best, but that's only because it had been such a long time since she'd made love. So long, in fact, that she'd forgotten how much she liked it. If she didn't know better, she'd have sworn making love with Dan was a whole different experience than anything she'd done before, but that was silly. The conversation at dinner, the suite, the atmosphere, all had conspired to transform the night into something magical. And face it, she really did like Dan. He was a terrific guy, and had it been a different time in her life...

Blah, blah, blah. She turned over and punched her pillow. It didn't help. Even she couldn't believe her own excuses. She liked the guy. She'd loved making love with him. She wanted more. Was it really possible to have Dan *and* her career? Could she have missed something along the way that would indicate she'd been all wrong?

She tried to think of one person, one woman who'd had

a satisfying love life in combination with a powerhouse career. Nothing off the top of her head, and when she finally did think of someone, an ad exec she'd met at a Woman in Marketing meeting, she remembered Estelle and her significant other lived in separate cities, her in New York, him in Los Angeles. Maybe that was the key—distance. Maybe she could set that up with Dan. If not actual distance, perhaps they could make a deal not to see each other but once every few months.

Turning over, she felt the first hope of the long night. That just might work. As long as they agreed not to call one another during the downtimes. Pretend that they honestly were separated by miles and miles.

The more she thought about it, the more it appealed. He would be a treat, a vacation, a reward for hard work. He could dive into his research projects, or take consulting jobs and not have to worry about a girlfriend. She could focus completely on her career moves and not be distracted.

She smiled. This just may be the best idea she'd ever had, better even than the concept for the New Dawn campaign.

Talk about having her cake and eating it too. This could solve everything.

The urge was to get up that second and rush into the living room. But she wasn't about to wake him. Besides, it was probably too soon to present the scenario. He might not see the beauty of the plan. She'd wait, see if the two of them continued to click as they had. But at least she didn't feel she had to keep him at arm's length. In fact, the more they bonded now, the easier it would be to get him with the program.

She sighed happily, found a comfy position, and let her mind drift. Life was good, and so was sex. Amen.

IT WASN'T THE LIMO Marla had expected. Instead, Shawn picked her up in a Yellow Cab, which was perfectly fine with her. He could have ridden up in a Rent-A-Wreck, and she'd have been happy.

He looked yummy in worn jeans and a kind of Mexican shirt, brown with white trim. His hair was a tiny bit damp, but still looked tantalizingly touchable. Marla pulled the door closed, and when she turned to him, his smile made her feel as if it was all her birthdays rolled up into one. And he was the present.

"You look wonderful," he said.

She rolled her eyes, even though she'd tried on every single item of clothing she owned before deciding on the forest-green jumper with the yellow-and-white blouse underneath. She didn't want to wear any of the fancy-shmansy clothes she'd bought for the parties, but she didn't want to be in torn jeans and a stretched-out T. "I wasn't sure where we were going," she said.

"You're perfect."

Her blush, she felt sure, was only the first of many. She couldn't help it. Blushing had always been her curse. Her face, it seemed, tried hard to match the exact shade of her hair. So far, she'd come darn close.

"So, uh, where are we going?"

"A deli I know. It's not fancy, but it's good."

"Ooh, yum. I love bagels and cream cheese."

"Great."

"And lox. Sometimes. As long as I don't put on too much. But just enough is great. With tomato and red onion."

"That's the way I like it, too."

"Really?"

He nodded.

Just then, the cabbie turned a corner, fast, and she fell right into his arms. Flustered, she tried to sit up, but found she couldn't.

"Don't move," he said.

When Marla looked up, it was right into his face, only inches away. "But—"

"I've been wanting to do this for a while," he whispered, and then he leaned down until his lips touched hers.

For a bit, all Marla could do was hold her breath and blink. But then the flashbulbs in her brain stopped, and she actually felt his lips, his gentle breath, his arms holding her close.

Her eyes fluttered shut as she abandoned herself to the moment. Sure, it was like someone else's life, but as long as she was borrowing it, she might as well enjoy herself.

Holy-moly, she'd never had many boyfriends before. Her geekdom in high school and college had assured her lack of dates. One time she'd been asked out by a drunk guy at a fraternity party who, it turned out, thought she was someone named Cristy, and that night ended with him throwing up all over her brand-new Skechers. As far as memories went, it pretty much sucked.

Now, this was truly the stuff memories should be made of. Shawn Foote, who was sweeter, smarter, funnier than she could have ever imagined, holding her. Kissing her.

She gasped as she felt his tongue swipe her front teeth, The gasp gave him the opening he was looking for, and in a moment that was seared into her brain for eternity, she tasted him. A hint of coffee, a little mint, and oh, God, Shawn!

She could die right now, and it would be fine. In fact, she kinda wished she would, because there was no possibility her life could get any better.

"Marla?"

She jumped just a tad when she saw he'd pulled back and was looking straight at her. "Hmm?"

"Is everything all right?"

She nodded. Three times.

"Just checking."

"No. Good. Happy."

He smiled. "That's excellent. But now we need to get out of the cab, because I think he's getting a little impatient."

They'd stopped, and she hadn't even known it. Oh, God. She sat up, ran a hand through her hair, cleared her throat, tried her best to climb down from the clouds that had carried her away.

By the time Shawn had paid the driver and gotten out, she was relatively together. Not Jessica together, but not her normal Marla self, either.

He took her hand, another keeper memory, and led her into the unassuming deli. She hardly felt the sidewalk beneath her feet.

DAN WOKE UP to knocking. Loud knocking. He'd slept like crap, and waking was no easy task. His gummy eyes refused to open, his legs were all tangled in the sheets, and whoever was knocking was about to die.

"Hold on," he said, but he doubted the knocker heard him.

Finally, Dan made it to his feet. He headed for the door, careful not to bump into anything. A swift glance to the bedroom door let him know that if Jessica had heard the door, she wasn't in any hurry to answer it.

Dan leaned forward and looked through the peephole. As he'd suspected, Owen, the bastard, was the one making all the racket. Just as Dan reached for the knob, ready to let Owen know exactly what he thought of him, he remembered the pullout couch. Shit. "Hold on," he said. "Just a second."

Dan raced to the bed, tossed the pillows to the side and shoved the bed back into the couch. It stuck, of course, just long enough for Owen to get impatient and start knocking again. The bed succumbed to brute pressure, and then he piled the pillows in random order. It was good enough. He leapt over the coffee table and made it back to the door before Owen beat a hole in the center. He jerked the door open. "Did you need something, Owen?"

Owen's unhappy gaze took in Dan's bare feet and boxer shorts. "I was hoping to speak to Jessica," he said, his words clipped tight.

"She's sleeping."

"She'll want to get up for me."

"I doubt it."

Owen sighed, shifted his stance so he was halfway to getting inside. Dan wasn't about to let that happen.

"Look, Owen, as soon as she's up, she'll give you a call."

"It's important."

"I'm sure it is. But we had a pretty rough night, if you know what I mean."

That got a reaction. Red-faced, Owen looked past Dan's shoulder, trying to see the bedroom door.

That was it. Not caring what he hit, Dan pushed Owen's shoulder with one hand while he closed the door with the other. "She'll call you."

"Hey!"

"I promise," he said as the door finally clicked home. "Jeez."

He turned around, not in the least happy about having to remake the bed. But man, he was still really tired. He'd left his watch on the coffee table, but he felt sure it was just past dawn.

Turned out it was almost noon, but hey.

"Was that Owen?"

Jessica's voice startled him, and he spun to find her standing by the open bedroom door. "Yeah."

"What did he want?"

"You."

"Oh." She hid a broad yawn behind her hand as she walked, kimono flaring behind her, to the bathroom.

Dan reacted to the sight in a way that belied his last encounter with her. Damn, she was so beautiful. Even with her hair all messed up, and makeup giving her that ever popular raccoon look. He wanted her just as she was. Well, okay, he could wait until she brushed her teeth, but barely.

He wondered which Jessica he'd be talking to this morning. The woman afraid to step a foot outside her comfort zone or the passionate creature he'd made love to. Maybe wishing real hard would help. Which is just what he did as he straightened up the pillows and gathered his clothes together. He stared at his robe for a long time, but he didn't put it on. If it was the passionate one, he wanted to be ready.

Talk about hopeful. She'd made it pretty clear last night that she wasn't terribly comfortable about testing the edges of their very personal envelope. He could either go along with it, be the nice guy he liked to think he was, or...

One thing of which he was quite sure: When they'd made love last night, Jessica had been right there with him, breath for breath, touch for touch. She'd come alive in his arms. God, it had been like nothing else. He wanted that woman back. He wanted to take that woman to the moon.

So much for Mr. Nice Guy. From this moment forward, he had a new project.

JESSICA HAD STARTED the shower the moment she'd stepped into the bathroom. She hadn't gotten wet yet, however. She'd dawdled over brushing her teeth, her hair, washing her face with New Dawn Creamy Facial Whip. She'd even taken off her robe and stared at herself in the mirror. All the while the hot water poured. She supposed she'd better make a decision. In or out.

One more critical view of her naked self. Not too shabby, although she could lose a few pounds, especially around her middle, but the personal trainer had been a great investment. She paid a fortune to her, but the money was excellent motivation. Now, if she could quit eating the damn desserts at every meal, maybe she'd get the body she should have.

It wasn't going to happen in the next five minutes though, so she'd better get on with it. She'd dawdled so long, Dan was undoubtedly dressed, but that was no matter. She'd never met a man who wouldn't strip at the drop of an innuendo.

After turning off the shower, she donned her robe, put her hand up to her mouth and blew out a breath, just to make sure, then went out to begin what she'd coined Project Dan. He wasn't the only one with a plan and a goal. And Jessica had always been great when it came to achievement. Give her a challenge and she was hell on wheels. So watch out, Mr. Research. The tide was going to turn, all her way.

"THIS IS THE BEST DELI I've ever been to," Marla said. "Except now I'm stuffed to the gills." She wiped her mouth with her napkin. "I never thought about it before, but that's about fish. Stuffing them, I mean. Otherwise it would be stuffed to the neck or the head."

Shawn put down his coffee cup and smiled at her. "I believe you're right. Never thought of it, either."

"Kind of disgusting, though."

"But it gets the message across."

She nodded. "How did you find this place?" It wasn't a big place, in fact it was not much more than a storefront. All the tables were taken, mostly with elderly folks, but by far the most popular area of the deli was the counter. Behind the glass were wonderful things, from fresh-baked ba-

gels to homemade knishes. Having grown up in a primarily
Jewish neighborhood, she was intimately familiar with the
delicacies. If she didn't have to go back to the hotel tonight,
she'd buy a bunch of goodies.

"What are you thinking about?"

"Kishke."

He laughed out loud, and the sound made her all twitchy
inside.

"What?"

"Not what I expected."

"But look at all the yummies," she said, pointing to the
counter. "I can't believe I'm so full. I mean, when's the
last time you saw such a beautiful black-and-white
cookie?"

"You're right. A work of art."

"Don't make fun."

His eyes widened as if he was wounded. "I'm not. Not
in the least. I love the way you think."

She frowned. "I think just like other people. Don't I?"

"No." He took her hand in his. "Not at all. Which is
terrific, so you'd better not get all worried about it."

"How can I help it? I mean, I know I'm not the brightest
person in the world, but I never thought I was that different."

"Different is only awful when you're a kid."

Shawn ran a single fingertip up the back of her hand,
making her whole body quiver.

"As soon as you're out of that wanting-to-be-like-
everyone-else phase, it's what you look for in new people.
The unique things. Good or bad, it's always interesting."

"Well, psychos are different."

"Yeah, you don't want to go too far, but I can't think
of anything worse than being just like everyone else."

"You're not. You're the most gorgeous guy on earth."

Shawn burst out laughing, while Marla turned three

shades of red. She couldn't believe she'd said that. If she could have found a hole to crawl into, she would have.

"Oh, babe, don't be embarrassed. That was totally sweet. And yeah, I did win the biological lottery, I'm aware of that. It's okay as long as I don't take myself too seriously."

"That's the thing, though. You don't. I never expected you to be so nice."

"Thought I'd be all stuck-up, huh?"

"Sure. I mean, beautiful people can get whatever they want. It must be easy to get sucked into that."

"Do you get whatever you want?"

"Me? What do you mean?"

He nodded. "You're incredibly beautiful."

"No, I'm not."

He leaned back to look at her sternly. "So I'm sweet, but I'm a liar?"

"No!"

"Then you'll just have to deal, won't you?"

She had no idea what to say. Not a clue. She was Alice Through the Looking Glass, Dorothy on the Yellow Brick Road. She felt sure she was going to wake up and realize it was all a dream, but she prayed it wouldn't happen yet. She was having way too much fun.

"Hey," Shawn said. "I have this party to go to tonight. At the Rainbow Room. How would you feel about being my date?"

"I have to go… Oh."

His slow smile made the whole world sunshiny. Her spot, especially. "I'd love to."

"Great. What time do you have to be there?"

A cloud appeared. "Early. Like two-ish."

"Ah. So how would you feel about starting this date around seven? When I get there?"

"I feel very, very good about this."

He leaned over and kissed her gently on the cheek. ''Remember,'' he whispered. ''The first dance is mine.''

Marla melted into a puddle of goo. Right there in front of the kosher dill pickles.

POINT OF VIEW

An English professor wrote the words "A woman without her man is nothing" on the blackboard and directed the students to punctuate it correctly.

The men wrote: "A woman, without her man, is nothing."

The women wrote: "A woman: without her, man is nothing."

Source: Meissner, Dirk "Punctuation and Phenomenal Women" http://www.dirkmeissner.com/chauvi0001.htm

13

SHE HADN'T GOTTEN dressed. A good sign. And she was smiling. Yet another favorable omen. But she also had a strange glint to her eyes, as if there was something wicked going on inside that formidable brain of hers.

"How'd you sleep?" she asked.

"Great. Never better. How about you?"

"Good, good."

He nodded, smiled. Not terribly sure what to say next, which wasn't something he was used to.

She walked over to the couch, sat on the opposite end. Crossing her legs, she let the robe fall so that her thigh was exposed. He couldn't tell if she had anything on beneath it.

"I can't believe Owen," she said. "He doesn't give up easily, does he?"

"Nope. He seemed pretty anxious to talk to you."

She frowned prettily. He liked her without makeup. It made him remember the feel of her skin.

"I'd better call him." She lifted the hotel phone, put it in her lap, then dialed his room number.

As she listened to her boss, she swung her upper leg, and his gaze traveled down to her feet. He wasn't exactly a foot man, although he knew at least one among his friends, but the way her toes looked with the red polish, the graceful curve of her arch sent some pretty interesting messages to the lower regions of his body.

He crossed his legs, regretting that he hadn't put on a

pair of jeans. He'd never really thought about how vulnerable it could be to be dressed only in boxers. Nice boxers, to be sure, silk, bought by his ex-girlfriend at Barney's, but still, they didn't leave a lot to the imagination.

"We'll be there at two," Jessica said, "and I'm sure that Theresa can fix everything. That's why we hired her. Nothing will go wrong tonight, I promise."

Dan moved his gaze from her feet to her ankles, trim and pale, up her well-shaped calf to the expanse of thigh. Somehow it was sexier than if she'd been completely undressed. Maybe not. The idea of her naked, sitting so casually on the couch, talking to that bastard of a boss, made his problem infinitely worse. He hoped she didn't ask him for a pen, or water, because standing would be mighty awkward.

"Dan was only thinking of me," she said. "He knows what a rough week this is, and how much I need my rest. I'm sure if your wife were here, she'd do the same."

He looked up to see Jessica smiling at him, a conspiratorial grin that made him think she'd gotten over her fear from last night. Perhaps he was too optimistic, but he didn't think so. It was an intangible something, along with the robe, the thigh. It added up.

Being the man of action that he was, he boldly scooted over on the couch. Not enough to actually touch her, but their hands could have met in the middle.

"I'll call Theresa, and I'll let you know if there's a problem, okay? If not, I'll see you at the Rainbow Room."

She hung up the phone and put it back on the coffee table. "Sorry about that."

"No sweat."

"I wanted to talk to you about last night." She paused, looked at her knee, then back at him. "I really had a great time."

"Yeah. Me, too."

"But I was a little frightened, too. I wasn't expecting it. You. It's been a long while since I..."

"I understand."

"I hope so. Because I wouldn't want you to think it was anything you'd done."

"Thanks."

"I'd like to buy you breakfast. What do you say?"

"Great. Where?"

She paused again, but this time she didn't look away. "Here."

"Oh."

"I don't have to be anywhere until two."

"Great."

Her smile turned up the heat about twenty degrees. "Maybe, after we eat, we can have dessert."

He tried to respond with something witty, but his brain had stopped functioning. Dessert. Oh, yeah. Maybe he could convince her to have dessert now and eat later.

PLEASANTLY FULL on eggs, bacon and toast, Jessica watched Dan take his last bites of Belgian waffle, wondering what she was going to do next.

The meal had been secondary to the mating dance they'd started just after she'd ordered from room service. Every word had been rife with meaning, and she couldn't help noticing that while Dan's boxers were a wonderful dark blue silk, they didn't do much to hide his enthusiasm. For that matter, her robe couldn't disguise the state of her nipples, brought to her attention by Dan's frequent stares.

The truth of the matter was that she was as excited as she could ever remember, her mind taking off in flights of erotic fantasy that grew more exotic as each minute passed. She was glad, however, that she'd insisted they eat. Not only was she fortified, but the tension had mounted and mounted. Now it was her turn. She giggled.

His eyebrows rose.

"Nothing," she said. "Just random odd thoughts."

"You don't want to share?"

She got up from the table and walked around in back of him. "I do. But not my silly thoughts."

Although he'd put on a bathrobe for the waiter, he'd taken it off as soon as the man had left, so he sat virtually naked. With so much wonderful flesh to explore, she wasn't sure where to start. Deciding at last, she ran both hands down his chest as she leaned forward, her breasts just touching the back of his head as she closed her eyes and let her fingers do the walking.

His sharp intake of breath was her first clue that she'd done good, and his pebbled nipples her second. She'd be willing to bet that his shorts were quite tight as she circled his nubs. She'd noticed last night that he was very sensitive there, something she could completely relate to.

"Jessica, my God. What you're doing to me." Dan's voice was hardly more than a growl as he stopped her torment by grasping her hands. He stood, turned around, put those same hands on either side of her face and came in for a long, slow, wet kiss.

He tasted of maple with a hint of coffee, and she felt sorry that she hadn't eaten something more exotically sweet. He didn't seem to mind.

With the satisfaction of her plan to bolster her courage, she opened her mouth freely to let him in, and in return she grew daring with her own ministrations.

He moved closer to her, rubbing against her, letting her feel what she was doing to him. It was amazing to know what was rubbing against her, to anticipate a rematch, this time with nothing to rein in her abandon.

Wanting Dan was a new experience, why exactly, she couldn't say. A combination of things, she supposed. His looks were but a small part of it, a delightful benefit.

Mostly, though, it was the man himself, his unique approach toward life, his strength, his passion.

As she thought the word, Dan moved his hands down to her belt and loosened it, letting her robe fall open.

It felt daring and wild to be naked like this. It wasn't the bedroom, and it wasn't at night, and his hands touched her breasts, cupping them gently, stealing her breath away.

"You're amazing," he whispered just before he nuzzled her ear. "So incredibly beautiful."

"So are you," she said, hardly aware of the words when her senses were under such sweet assault.

He kissed down her chest until he reached her right nipple, which he took between his teeth, not biting, just holding. Then his tongue flicked very fast, like a lizard's, focusing on the incredibly sensitive flesh, and she arched her neck with pleasure.

Her hands went to his hair, raking her fingers in the soft strands, gripping him to hold herself steady as he moved to her left breast to repeat his torment.

Then, just when she thought she couldn't stand another minute, he fell to his knees in front of her.

He kissed the flat of her tummy, then just below. His hands moved to her thighs, applying gentle pressure so she spread them. Knowing what he was about to do made her quiver with anticipation, but he was not to be rushed. He continued his slow descent, swirling his tongue on her bare skin, tasting her, nipping her with his teeth.

All she could do was moan and hold on as he reached her lips. Kneeling there before her, she gasped as his wicked tongue entered her, taking long, slow licks, his own moan merging with hers.

He didn't dawdle; instead, he found her clit and mimicked his trick with his teeth, taking the tiny bud with infinite care, then flicking, flicking, giving her goose bumps, making her tremble, coaxing loud gasps as he went on and on, unrelenting until, in less time than she thought possible, she cried out with an orgasm that shook her to her toes.

So violent were her spasms that he lost his grip, and when she finally opened her eyes, still gulping great drafts of air, she found him staring up at her, watching as if it was the most fascinating and wonderful thing he'd ever seen.

"Oh my God," she whispered. Her body continued to shake, and she realized with a guilty start that she still had his hair in her fists. She let go, but before she could apologize, Dan was on his feet. The next second, he ran his hands down her sides until he cupped the back of her thighs, then she was up in his arms, her legs wrapped around his back, her arms hanging on to his neck.

He kissed her as he walked her backward, the taste of him her taste, sultry, dark, erotic.

A moment later and her back hit the wall, cold even through the silk of her robe.

He looked at her, his eyes smoky and dangerous. "Come again," he whispered. "Let me watch you. Come."

Then she felt the hard pressure of his penis as he searched for her opening. When he found it, he thrust in so hard, her head hit the wall, but she didn't even feel it. She was too busy gasping at the incredible sensation of fullness, of perfection.

Then, bracing them both, he started his assault, slowly at first, building in speed and pressure. The way he rubbed her, by some delightful fluke of nature, his length slid over her swollen clit, in seconds wringing out another climax, stronger, if possible, than the first.

His gaze never wavered, his eyes never closed, and she struggled to keep from closing her own. They stared into each other's souls as he pushed into her over and over, faster and faster, until finally, he cracked, and every muscle in his body, in his face, tightened to fever pitch, and then he cried out, a long, low guttural cry of release.

After several quavering breaths, he opened his eyes again. He kissed her, the fever still in him, but waning. She could feel his trembling as much as her own as he stepped back, guiding her to her feet.

She wasn't terribly steady. Holding on to his arm, he walked her over to the couch, where they both sat, catching their breaths.

He held her hand. The simple gesture struck her as impossibly tender. They didn't speak, didn't need to. A single thought repeated over and over in her mind. Perfection. Her plan was perfect. She could live a long time on memories of this. Anticipating this. When they finally did get together, it would be fireworks and earthquakes. Yes, it was the very essence of perfection.

She lifted his hand to her lips, kissed him gently, and whispered the word aloud.

HE'D SPENT the afternoon taking a long nap. It was hard to believe she had to work. If she felt anything close to what he did, she must be a wreck. After that earthshaking encounter after breakfast, they'd showered together, and things had led to things. He was pretty damn proud of himself. Tired, but proud.

He'd decided to eat some dinner at a nearby Mexican joint, careful not to dirty his tuxedo. Afterward, it was a quick cab to Rockefeller Center, and the hoopla at the Rainbow Room.

The guests wouldn't begin to arrive for another thirty minutes, so it was a little tricky getting past security, but finally they paged Jessica, and she came down to meet him.

Stunning again, this time in a dress that was to his eye pink, but she informed him it was actually ashes of roses.

Whatever. She looked like a million bucks, and he felt like the king of the world walking into the venerable old club.

Some things never change, and for that he was grateful. The Rainbow Room still had that thirties art deco look, with a revolving dance floor, killer views of the city, including the Empire State Building, and the best damn bands the country had to offer. Tonight, one of his favorites: Harry Connick and his Big Band. Gotta love it.

"I've missed you," he said as soon as they were out of earshot of any roving workers.

She smiled. "Believe me, I would have preferred to stay at the hotel."

"Uh-oh. Owen?"

She nodded. "He's shadowing me, regaling me nonstop with tales of your unbelievable rudeness. He suggested most strongly I should break up with you. Actually, I think he wants me to dump you in the East River with a block of concrete, but breaking up would suffice."

"I have to say this for him, he's consistent."

"That's for sure. I just wish he would stop being such a consistent jerk."

"I'll do my best to keep him off your scent, but it's not going to be easy." He leaned forward and nuzzled her neck. "You smell so damn good."

She ran her hand down his neck. They turned at the same moment to meet in a kiss that reminded him just how lucky he was.

"How long do we have to stay at this shindig?"

"Till the bitter end."

"Suppose anyone would notice if I, say, hit the fire alarm in about an hour?"

"Cute." Jessica kissed him quickly on the mouth. "Very cute. But I need you to be a good boy. Go find my boss and neuter him, okay?"

"Yes, ma'am."

"I'll find you when I can."

"Oh, goody."

She sighed.

"One thing, though. You owe me a dance. I didn't get the last one, and I won't leave without it tonight. Especially on that revolving dance floor."

"All right. I promise. Now I have to get back to work."

"I know. But think of me."

Touching his sleeve lightly, her expression grew sad. "That's all I've been doing. Which isn't so good. I need this week to be perfect."

He touched her chin, lifting her face until her gaze met his. "We're fine," he said. "So you can safely put me on the shelf until it's convenient to bring me out again. I won't mind. And I'm not going anywhere."

"Thank you," she said, and he could see she meant it. "I'll try. But you're not that easy to forget."

"I'm trying hard to see how that's bad. No, I'm kidding. I mean it. The place looks fantastic, you're the most beautiful woman in New York, and everyone in America and beyond is going to rush out and buy New Dawn cosmetics. So just go with the flow, my love. You'll be perfect."

Jessica kissed him one more time, only this time she lingered. When she walked away, he had to fight the urge to follow.

Better instead to use this energy to find Owen. The little weasel.

JESSICA STOOD at the edge of the floor-to-ceiling glass windows, but her gaze wasn't on the spectacular view. She watched the dance floor, the banquet tables, the bars, as the crowd enjoyed the festivities. Even she had to admit, this was one hell of a bash.

The room, maybe the most elegant in Manhattan, sparkled. The walls and floors had a rich and subdued color scheme with full-length mirrors between narrow wall panels covered in brown satin. The emerald-green carpets blended perfectly with the jade-green leather-upholstered chairs. Mirrors, crystal, especially the magnificent chandelier above the dance floor, made everything and everyone in the space radiant.

The slide show, running continuously on the wide screen above the bandstand, was the best she'd seen of its kind, worth the incredible hours of hard work she'd put into it. New Dawn was having one hell of a send-off, and the movers and shakers of Manhattan were all in attendance.

From where she stood, she could see Oprah, John Travolta and his beautiful wife Kelly Preston, Chris Noth, Barbara Walters, Kate Hudson, Gwen Stefani, Marla and Shawn, and a host of *InStyle* magazine regulars. But none of them held her attention; she only had eyes for one man.

There he was. At the edge of the bar, staring right at her. The sexiest guy in the room.

He lifted a martini glass in tribute, drank a bit, then put it carefully on the bar behind him. Then he headed toward her, artfully dodging dancers, drinkers, models, reporters, waiters. The nearer he came, the faster her heart beat. Everything about him; the way he looked in his tux, the insouciant lock of hair, the very way he moved, all grace and raw sex appeal, made her feel as if this was her first date. It was crazy, really, for it to hit her so hard, so fast, but it was utterly undeniable.

He passed the last barrier to join her by the window. He lifted her hand and kissed the back. "I believe we have this dance."

She glanced at the bandstand. "There's no music."

"There will be."

She couldn't say no, but she did hope real hard that she wouldn't make a complete fool of herself. She had a seriously limited sense of rhythm. She could keep the tempo of anything by John Philip Sousa, but beyond that, she was rather hopeless. Dancing was mostly to be avoided. But tonight she wouldn't dream of it.

Because the band had taken a break, they were alone on the dance floor. All around them, the room buzzed with conversation and laughter. None of it penetrated their cocoon.

He put his arms around her, drew her to him. Her cheek went to his chest as she snuggled close. They stood quite still while she counted his heartbeats, and in an act of magic, her rhythm became his rhythm, her breath, his.

To complete the moment, to honor his promise…music.

The song was that lovely Hoagy Carmichael tune "The Nearness of You," so romantic that it carried her on wings. He led, she followed, and together they were exquisite grace.

When she lifted her chin to look at him, she realized he was singing, very softly. That he knew every word. Not just that, oh, no. She knew that every word was meant as a promise from him to her. For this dance. For this night. For…

Why Men Are Happy To Be Men

1) Phone conversations are over in thirty seconds flat.

2) A five-day vacation requires only one suitcase.

3) You can open all your own jars.

4) If you are thirty-four and single, nobody notices.

5) Same work...more pay.

Source: PLiG "Being a Bloke"
http://plig.org/things/beingabloke.html

14

Too tired to make love when they got back to the hotel at three, Jessica did pull him with her into the bedroom. "Is this okay?"

He nodded. "More than okay." He kissed her, then brushed her cheek with the back of his hand. "Go do your stuff," he said. "I'll wait."

She smiled with an effort, not because she didn't appreciate his gentlemanly behavior, but because she was just too exhausted.

When she got back from the bathroom, Dan had stripped down to his shorts, a nice silk plaid. She thought about the last time she'd seen him in boxers. They certainly hadn't fit him that loosely.

How was it possible to feel so aroused when she was ready to drop. Strange, strange.

By the time he got back to the bedroom, she was tucked beneath the comforter, wearing nothing at all. Normally, she slept in a nightshirt, but she wanted to feel Dan next to her.

God, how he'd made her feel tonight. Like a princess. Like the luckiest person in the world.

She'd seen how the women at the party had looked at him. Enviously. Greedily. Even the most glamorous and celebrated of the party guests had coveted her.

In one way, it made her feel smug, powerful. But the attention was also a bit intimidating. When people looked at them, she wasn't who they were looking at.

"Hey," he said as he crawled in beside her. "Did I mention how much fun I had with you tonight?"

She nodded. "A few times."

"Did I forget to say that you were the most beautiful woman there?"

"Uh, nope."

He turned on his side, putting his arm around her waist. "How about that I'll never forget dancing with you? That you made me feel like Fred Astaire?"

"Me? You're the one who can dance. I can't believe I didn't step all over your feet."

"Nonsense. You were an angel with wings."

"And you're full of baloney."

He got that shocked look on his face. "You wound me."

"You'll survive."

His eyes softened as he leaned forward to kiss her chin. "You should probably know that if I had an ounce of energy left in my body, I'd be ravaging you about now."

"And you should know if I could stay awake, I'd be letting you."

"Okay, then."

"Right."

He kissed her again, but not on the chin. This one lasted a lot longer, too. But finally, he pulled back, she settled down, and they slept, their bodies nestled together like spoons.

MARLA WALKED into the hotel pressroom to find Jessica talking with the editor in chief of *Glamour*. Listening without looking like an eavesdropper, she couldn't help admiring Jessica's aplomb, her ease, her wit. Marla still wanted to grow up to be just like her. But before she got all adult and stuff, she was champing at the bit to tell her boss everything that had happened in the last few days. Not the

work stuff, because Jessica knew all that, but the Shawn
stuff.

In the meantime, Marla checked in with Cord Wilson,
who, with his team, staffed the press booth. They were in
charge of tonight's shindig, a press party aboard a boat that
would cruise along the Hudson River. Marla was going, of
course, and so was Shawn.

Just thinking his name made her sigh.

"What's wrong?"

Marla spun around to find Jessica right behind her. "Oh,
I thought you were with the *Glamour* editor in chief."

"We're finished. Why did you sigh like that? Are you
okay?"

"Oh, yeah. Very, very okay."

Jessica smiled. "I gathered that last night."

"Really? You saw us? I mean, you saw he was, like,
talking to me, and we were kinda together. Like a date?"

"Yes, I saw. Now, we must go to the bar and discuss
this situation, yes?"

Marla nodded. "Oh, yes. Definitely."

DAN FINISHED checking his phone messages, then turned
on his computer to retrieve his e-mail. He'd have a ton of
it, but most was probably spam.

As his computer downloaded, he got the phone and
called his mother.

She answered with her typical cheer.

"Hi, Mom. How's it going?"

"Your cat peed in my shoes."

"Really? I've been training her for months. Be sure and
give her an extra treat."

"Ha, ha. Now, how are you, and how is the big experiment going?"

"Great and great."

"No kidding? I figured she'd get tired of you and throw you out after the second night."

"Gee, your faith in me is touching."

"Only you would think prying into some strange girl's private thoughts is a romp in the park. Private thoughts are private for a reason. Wasn't it Oscar Wilde who said, 'There is hardly anyone whose sexual life, if it were broadcast, would not fill the world at large with surprise and horror'?"

"No. It was Somerset Maugham. However, I don't find anything Jessica does horrible. Surprising, yes, but not horrible."

"Oh, my."

Dan realized he couldn't do the e-mail and talk at the same time, so he brought up his solitaire game. That he could practically do with his eyes closed. "What's that supposed to mean?"

"You've fallen for her. Three days out of the gate, and you're in love."

"Don't be ridiculous. I'm not in love."

"You are. And she's going to break your heart."

"She is not."

"Aha!"

"Don't aha me. She's a very bright, very insightful woman, and she's illuminating the subject in a way I never anticipated."

"Which means," his mother said, her voice dropping an octave, "that you've stopped asking questions and are just having sex as often as humanly possible."

Dan opened his mouth to protest, when it occurred to him that his mother was right. He hadn't asked Jessica anything for what, twenty-four hours? "Shit."

"Oh, honey. What can I tell you? Your intentions are always so good, but when it comes to women…"

"What?"

"Let's just say that famous scientific detachment comes unglued."

The solitaire game forgotten, Dan leaned forward in his chair. "You don't understand, Mom, she's different."

"Right."

"No, really. She's doing a bang-up job on this marketing campaign. She's focused but not obsessive, and she's been unbelievably honest with me. That's why it seems like it's moving so fast, because we're smashing through all the typical getting-to-know-each-other bullshit."

"I understand."

"I know that tone of voice," he said, getting a little fed up. "You're assuming a hell of a lot."

Silence on the other end of the line. Then finally, just as he was going to apologize, his mother did.

"I'm sorry. You're right. I have no business judging you like this. For what it's worth, sweetheart, I hope she's everything you ever dreamt of."

"I'm not saying she's that," he said, hating the defensiveness he heard in his voice. "I'm just saying she's, you know, great."

"Good. And when am I going to see you?"

"After it's all over. Next weekend, I guess."

"So your cat will have every opportunity to pee in all the rest of my shoes."

"Oh, don't worry about that. I also trained her to pee in your sock drawer."

"Daniel!"

"I love you, Mom. Talk to you soon."

He hung up to the sound of her sputtering. His smile didn't last, however. He stood up, went to his window and stared at the street below. Was he rushing into this? Was he making Jessica into something she wasn't? Or was this excitement that he'd felt since that first day something real, something he could count on?

So he hadn't asked any questions. That was just a matter of timing, nothing more. He'd ask. He had by no means abandoned his project. On the contrary. Knowing her this well was a stunning revelation. Hadn't he been spot-on about her fear after that first time? By giving her space, she'd come around by the next morning. That proved that he was starting to understand women!

And he also understood that he'd better get his ass in gear if he wanted to get dressed and make it out to the boat by five.

MARLA SIPPED her mocha Frappuccino noisily as she hit bottom. For the last forty minutes, she'd been talking a mile a minute, telling Jessica every last detail about her and Shawn. Jessica had never seen Marla so animated, so over the moon. There simply wasn't a way to stay passive in the face of so much happiness.

And still, Jessica couldn't help wondering what was going to happen when the week was over. Shawn was a famous man, with a whole world full of women to choose from. While Jessica thought Marla was one of the best, brightest, and certainly sweetest, did Shawn Foote really want her for keeps? Watching Marla talk, with her extravagant gestures and her totally unique vocabulary, all Jessica could think was if Shawn hurt Marla, she would chase him down and cut him where it hurts the most.

"And he said that he wants me to come with him to Montana. He's thinking about buying the ranch that's right next to Harrison Ford's. I mean, can you imagine? 'Uh, Harrison,' she said, lowering her voice in an approximation of no one in particular, 'May I borrow a cup of sugar? Or maybe an Oscar?'"

"Did Harrison Ford win an Oscar?"

"I'm not sure, but I don't think we'll be borrowing it anyway."

"True." Jessica sipped her plain old coffee. "Montana, huh?"

"What's not to like?" Marla said. "I mean, trees, horses, cows. Woodland creatures. Bunnies!"

"Right. Deer."

"Bambi!"

"Oh, does Shawn hunt?"

Marla looked stricken, but only for a moment. "Don't know. Can't imagine. He's too sweet to shoot anything. I think he fishes, though."

"Fishing's okay."

"Yeah. As long as, you know, you eat them."

"Right."

"And you don't have to look into their eyes."

Jessica nodded, understanding completely. In fact, she understood a lot about what her assistant was feeling. More than she liked to admit.

What Jessica had that Marla didn't, however, was her plan. Even though she hadn't stopped thinking of Dan since this morning, that wasn't because she was getting all "gooey" about him, as Marla would say. She was simply reacting to the novelty of such great sex.

"Aha!" Marla said, pointing straight at Jessica.

"What?"

"I knew it. You're also sharing this wonderfulness with your handsome Dan. It's happening to us both!"

"Wait a minute," Jessica said, feeling her cheeks heat and fighting the urge to bolt. "It's not what you think."

Marla's eyes widened and Jessica realized what she'd almost admitted.

Marla leaned forward. "He's not really a boyfriend from college, is he?"

She kept her expression completely neutral, despite the blush she couldn't hide. "Of course he is."

"Oh. I thought he was someone you brought to get

Creepy Owen to back off because, well, you not having a life and all.'' Now it was Marla's turn to blush. "I didn't mean that the way it sounded."

"It's okay," Jessica said. "I'm not offended. I work hard at maintaining that image."

"Why?"

"Because personal lives get so messy."

"Hmm."

Jessica hated it when Marla did that. Got all quiet and wouldn't look her in the eye. "Come on. Out with it."

"Well, it's only my opinion."

"Yes?"

"Doesn't it make your happiness dependent on your job? And wasn't it you who told me, early on, that companies have no loyalty to anything but the bottom line?"

"My career doesn't depend on one job."

"True, but it does depend on some job. And that's not very comforting, is it?"

"Marla? Go buy yourself another Frappuccino, would you?"

"Okay. But then we have to go get dressed. It's boat time tonight."

"Yes, it is," Jessica said, amazed she hadn't blown it. At least not completely.

"Dan will be there, right?"

She nodded.

"Oh, goody. You'll have fun."

Jessica said nothing, not as Marla got up, or even when she put her hand on her shoulder. It did occur to her that in all the time they'd worked together, it was the first time they'd actually touched like that. Jessica couldn't help wondering if it was because Marla had changed, or she had.

THE NICE THING about the boat trip was that someone other than Jessica was in charge. Which didn't mean she could just sit around and drink mai tais, but she wasn't responsible for the whole gig.

The bad thing about the boat trip was that Jessica wasn't exactly the warm bubbly woman he'd kissed on his way out this morning. It wasn't like that first night, when she'd gotten so scared. But she also wasn't the open book.

For his part, he was pretty determined to get back on track. Not that he wasn't going to continue to make all that hot monkey love to her, but he was going to refocus on the project.

Once she came back from talking to some *People* magazine bigwig, he would ask away. If he could figure out what to ask, that is.

"May I refill that drink?"

He looked up into the pretty eyes of the cocktail waitress. She was the opposite of Jessica in almost every way, from her blond hair to her tall, too-thin body. But her smile was nice and friendly. "Yes, please. And bring a whiskey sour, would you?"

"Of course, sir." She headed off, but he found her looking back at him twice.

It hadn't skipped his notice that ever since he'd started this job, women had been coming on to him. A lot. Way more than normal. In fact, he could go weeks, months, without being the recipient of that kind of smile. But every time he was with Jessica, he was a babe magnet. What was with that?

"Hi." Jessica sat down across from him. She breathed deeply then exhaled as she pushed her hair behind her ear. "That woman is a barracuda," she said. "It's like she wants New Dawn to fail. Maybe she doesn't like cosmetics. Or maybe she just doesn't like me."

"That's absurd. How could anyone not like you?"

Jessica looked at him a long time. In fact, he was getting a little worried when she finally said, "I don't care."

"What?"

"I don't care if people like me. I don't understand why I even said that. I need them to buy the product I'm selling, that's all. Or promote it, or whatever else they need to do for me to succeed. Liking me has nothing to do with it."

He wasn't sure what brought this on, and decided to keep his mouth shut.

"I don't want people to hate me, either. What I mean is, it shouldn't matter. I'm not in a popularity contest. What she thinks of me is no concern of mine."

"Okay."

She looked him in the eye critically. "Do me a favor, would you, Dan?"

"Anything."

"Let's cut the intimate act when we're in public, unless Owen is right there, okay? I need to keep my eye on the prize, and that's not going to happen if I'm dancing with you all night."

Her words hit him like a blow. All he could do was nod, smile, act as if it meant nothing. As if this was just another day at the office. As if what she felt about him was no concern of his.

Top Five Things Only Women Understand

5. *Fat clothes.*

4. *Cutting your bangs to make them grow.*

3. *Romantic stuff like mushy cards and flowers.*

2. *The inaccuracy of every bathroom scale ever made.*

1. *Other women!!!*

Source: Dobhran "Top Ten Things Only Women Understand"
http://www.dobhran.com/humor/

15

JESSICA COULDN'T believe it. Here she was, in the middle of another tremendously successful party, getting raves from everyone from *E!* to *W,* accolades up the ying-yang from the folks at New Dawn, the wink-wink-nudge-nudge from Revlon, Chanel and Estée Lauder, and all she could think about was Dan.

She'd hurt him, which she hadn't meant to, but now that it was done, and the repercussions were in progress, maybe she *had* meant to hurt him, to send the whole business back to square one. She wanted to start over, to put on the brakes well before she'd become entranced, definitely before they'd become intimate. But some things can't be undone, can't be unfelt.

She looked over at Dan, standing by the bar, toying with his drink. He'd had a few, more than was probably wise, but she wouldn't dream of saying a word. He'd taken her at her word, and he'd backed off completely until Owen had approached. Then it was as if nothing had changed. Dan had become affectionate, endearing, territorial. She had to admit it had felt incredibly good, which was, of course, the problem.

She'd felt so sure about the plan of hers, to see Dan every few months, wear each other out in the bedroom, then do it again in another few months. It still felt as if that was the way to go. But talking to Marla had put a kink in the works, and Jessica wasn't quite sure why.

The only way the plan was going to work was if she and

Dan didn't expect too much from each other. It totally depended on the focus being sex. She didn't want more than that. In fact, she wasn't even sure at this stage of the game if she could handle that much.

She wasn't sure why, but sex always seemed to be more than sex for women. Men usually had the right idea, but women wanted more. Romance, security, love, commitment, a future. Why? Why wasn't it okay to want sex for its own sake?

It would be enough for her, but only if there were no expectations of anything else. No hoping, no plotting, no daydreaming. All her thoughts needed to be on work, and her creativity, too. She wanted to rise to the top of a very competitive market, and to do that she needed focus, focus, focus.

How could she do that when she was worried about Dan's feelings being hurt? Maybe if she just explained things to him, set it all out like the business proposition she had in mind, he'd sign on, and they wouldn't have to continue to go through this emotional crap. It was too draining. And too distracting.

She simply wouldn't worry about him anymore tonight. Tomorrow, when they had some privacy, she'd lay out the ground rules and see if he wanted to play.

"UH, DAN? Is everything okay?"

He looked up from his drink to see Marla standing to his immediate left, so pretty in her sailor dress, complete with a little blue boat pin on the collar. "I'm fine," he said.

"Not that we know each other that well or anything, but that's a total lie."

He had to smile. They hadn't spent a lot of time talking, but he was enchanted by the way she spoke. "Not a total lie. Just a partial lie."

"Which part?"

"Just the part before the period."

"Ah. Anything you want to talk about?"

"No."

"Oh, okay."

"Except, maybe you can help me."

She moved next to him, putting her right elbow on the bar, her left foot on the rail, mimicking his stance exactly. "I'll do my best."

"What is it with women?"

She raised both eyebrows, pursed her lips, but at least she didn't burst out laughing. "I don't know. Can you narrow that down any?"

He sipped his drink, surprised yet again that he wasn't drunker. Usually his limit was two, on a bad night three. This was his fourth screwdriver. He remained disappointingly sober. "Narrow it down? Okay. Let's try this. Why do women think it's perfectly fine to change their minds every twenty seconds? First it's yes, then it's no, then it's maybe, then back to yes, then *damn* no. Are you starting to see the drift here or should I continue?"

"Perfectly clear," Marla said, nodding so her red hair flowed down past her shoulders, then back up. "I'm familiar with the pattern."

"So? What's the deal? Why can't women say yes and mean yes?"

"Sometimes they do."

"When? When exactly do they do that? What in hell does it take to make a woman mean what she says? I don't get it."

Marla patted his shoulder. "It must be frustrating. But it's not personal."

"It sure as hell feels personal."

"Personal is usually when she says no and means no."

"You're saying rejection is final."

"Almost all the time."

"Almost?"

"Yeah, see, because there might be new information."

"I'm not talking about court proceedings here. I'm talking about—" He stopped, unwilling to get more detailed about the situation. He was still working for Marla's boss.

"It's tricky when you're talking about…stuff. Because with…stuff, there are a lot of factors. When women do say yes, they usually mean yes forever, so there aren't many casual yeses. And sometimes women can think that they're saying yes to one thing and then realize it's a completely other thing they've said yes to, and then they're not sure about the yes, so that's when the maybe comes into play. But the no, that's typically pretty clear, except when the no is because the woman is frightened about a new situation, and so she says no, but that really doesn't mean no, it's mostly a maybe, but the man, he needs to give her time to see that there's nothing to be afraid of, and that she won't ruin her career because she falls in love."

Dan blinked twice. Shockingly, he'd understood everything Marla had said, specifically that last bit. "Okay, so let's say some men get it about the being afraid part, and some men make allowances for that which seem to work but not really. Then what?"

"Keep trying?" she asked, her voice going way up high.

"But when is it real stupid for a man to keep trying? How does a man know when no is no and yes is yes?"

"That one I can sort of help with."

"Oh?"

She nodded. "There's a yes that when you hear it, you know that it's a forever yes. It's different from a maybe yes, and definitely different from a no yes."

He looked at his vodka. Maybe he was drunk. "You're sure about this."

"Absolutely. So don't worry about it. It takes time to get to the forever yes."

He didn't dare look at her, so he kept studying his drink. "What if I'm not sure I'm ready for a forever yes?"

"Then it's good that it's not here yet. Just be patient." She touched his arm with two fingers. "She's worth it."

He met her sympathetic gaze. "Am I?"

She leaned over and kissed his cheek. "I'd like to think so. But only you can answer that question."

"Where's your guy?"

Her face changed completely, lighting up from the inside. "He's busy with one of the photographers, but he's going to come get me when he's done."

"You seem pretty happy with him."

"I am. He's so wonderful. And interesting, and funny. Sweeter than anyone, and I love that he's so much more than just his looks, you know? Not that his looks aren't incredible, but he's so much more than that. He's got all these plans for the future and he doesn't buy into all the artificial junk about modeling and stuff. I don't know, he's just…"

He smiled, happy for her. "Yeah."

"Yeah."

"I want to say be careful."

"Careful? How is that possible? To be careful means not caring all the way. Not opening my heart. Then you wouldn't know. And it would be too easy to miss out on the one thing that could be the most important thing of all."

The band started again, playing "String of Pearls," a Glenn Miller tune, as Marla walked away. Dan wished the boat ride was over. He needed time to think. He liked so much about Jessica, but was it love? Was his mother right about him? He'd always been a romantic and it had gotten him into trouble time and time again. Maybe this was just the same old, same old. Maybe he wasn't really seeing Jessica for who she was, but as some amalgam of who he wanted her to be.

For sure, he'd never experienced anything even close to the experience of making love to her. And when they talked, there was a rightness to the conversations. He felt good with her, wanted to know more about her.

Maybe backing off was the right thing. Goddamn it, this was crazy. He'd never equivocated like this, not over any woman. Not over anything for that matter.

He no longer wanted to find out what women wanted. He wanted only to find out what one specific woman wanted. The question was, how?

THE NIGHT ENDED, at least for Jessica, just after midnight. Because she wasn't officially in charge of the event, she didn't have to stay to the bitter end.

Owen had hovered, of course, when she'd said good-night, and Dan had risen to the occasion once again. Attentive, respectful, charming. Everything she could hope for in a date, real or not.

They walked down to the pier, arm in arm, smiling, their bodies touching with each step. She felt the same shimmer of excitement that had been the constant since that first day. It was as if when they touched, they completed an electrical current. No one else did it to her. She'd never known it was possible.

They reached the street and got in line to wait for a cab. She turned to him. "What is it that you like about me?" she asked.

The question clearly took him by surprise. "Is this a test?"

"No. Think of it as research. Come on, what appeals?"

"There are a lot of things."

"Name five."

"Okay," he said, stretching the word. Let's see…"

"Nothing? Not one thing comes to mind?"

"No, no. Oh, God, no. Give me a second to get my thoughts together, that's all."

"And it can't be about sex."

His face fell. "Oh."

She elbowed him. "I can't believe—"

"I'm kidding, I'm kidding. Come on. You're…"

She stepped back, waiting.

His eyes softened and he touched her cheek with the back of his hand. "I like your drive, your intensity. You're honest, and you make no bones about who you are and what you want. You certainly come up with creative solutions to your problems." He nodded toward the boat. "This whole campaign is brilliant."

Jessica frowned. "That's it?"

A laugh escaped. "That's it? I've just described an amazing woman."

"But what about me?"

"I don't understand."

She turned, embarrassed by the sudden rush of tears. "I like to think I'm nice. That I have a sense of humor. You know, human things."

"Oh, Jessica," he whispered as he pulled her into his arms. "You're all that. Funny and nice, and so much more. Marla adores you and wants to be just like you. I see how people talk to you, with respect, with ease. You don't intimidate, you make people feel welcome and comfortable. Even that first time we met, at the bar, you were so willing to dive into my insane scheme. Willing to open yourself to a stranger. Don't you see how remarkable that is?"

Her head rested on his chest, but she shook it anyway. "I was so mean to you tonight."

"No you weren't. You were just honest."

"It's not your fault. You've never pressured me, or made any demands."

"Oh, but I have. And I'm going to demand more. I've

decided we need to go back to our original agreement. I ask you questions, and keep Owen at bay. You answer questions, and you concentrate on getting through this week with all your energy and strength. Whatever I can do to help, I'll do. If that means leaving you the hell alone, then fine. Just say the word.''

Now she lifted her head to meet his gaze. Amazed, once more, at this odd, beautiful man. Unlike anyone in her experience, and yet she felt as if she'd known him for a long, long time. She rose on her toes, stretched her neck, but she couldn't reach him. He smiled slowly and leaned down until his lips touched hers.

The shock of his kiss swept through her again, and for once in her life she turned off that part of her brain that analyzed everything, weighed every move. She just kissed him. A boy, a girl, a moonlit night.

A long, sweet, melting kiss.

THEY RODE BACK to the hotel in silence, comfortable, touching.

Dan had meant what he said, that he would step back, not make this more complicated than it needed to be. Jessica had enough on her plate without him adding to it.

There would be time, later, to explore the connection, the desire he felt for her. For now, he would appreciate what he had and not beg for more.

Once inside the suite, he guided her to the bedroom, then shut the door behind her. Knowing she would be a few minutes, he undressed quickly in the bathroom, brushed his teeth and cleared out. She tiptoed past as he made the couch into his bed. Despite his intentions, it wasn't fun when she waved good-night and closed the bedroom door behind her.

But it was better this way. He needed to figure out what he wanted, and so did she. The sex, while fantastic, made things difficult, confusing.

He turned off the lights and climbed into bed. Putting his hands behind his head, he stared up at the ceiling for a long time, seeing nothing but dark. His thoughts went in circles, always coming back to being inside her. Why was it so unique? She wasn't shaped differently, she hadn't come up with some new and wild technique. Yet with her it was…

Shit. He didn't know what it was. Great wasn't the half of it. It changed him. How, he couldn't explain. But it was true nonetheless. If it was still so after this week, then he could take the time to fully explore the reasons. As for now, he had to forget about making love to her. If he could. It was certainly asking a lot.

He closed his eyes, needing to sleep, knowing sleep was going to prove elusive. But he tried.

The moments ticked on, the night grew still and vast. He listened to the sound of his own heartbeat, trying to slow it down, but having no success.

Then he heard a new sound, the bedroom door opening. Whatever progress he'd made with his heart was shot to hell as his hopes rose. She was probably just going to the bathroom, nothing more. Besides, hadn't he just gone on and on about stepping back? Putting sex aside?

Her footsteps were lost in the thick carpet, and he couldn't place her in the room. That is, until he saw her shadow on the wall.

He turned his head, and there she was, made somehow silver by the light of the moon. She approached the bed slowly, quiet as a mouse, until she stood not a foot away, right next to the bed.

He could just see her expression. Worried. In fact, she was chewing on her lower lip.

Dan threw back the covers. Jessica sat down, making the slim mattress curve under her weight.

"I couldn't sleep," she whispered.

"Lie down."

"You said you didn't want to."

"I know."

"I said I didn't want to."

He smiled, knowing she couldn't see him. "I know."

"But here I am."

He reached out with his hand, grasped hers and squeezed. "Come," he said.

"Are you sure?"

"No."

"What if it's a huge mistake?"

He gave her a little tug. "Then let's make it together."

She nodded, then slowly stretched out next to him. He closed his eyes, achingly aware of the softness of her skin, of the way her hip felt against his, of her closeness, her scent.

"You know there's a basic problem with your project," she said.

"What's that?"

"The premise. How can you ever understand women, when we don't understand ourselves?"

He turned over on his side, and looked down into her shadowy face. "I don't believe it. I think you understand every mystery in the universe. That you know all the secrets of the heart. You just have to listen to your own wisdom, that's all."

Her hand moved up to the back of his neck. "Is this wise?"

He answered her with a kiss.

What Women Really Mean

1. *Do what you want — You'll pay for this later.*

2. *We need to talk — I need to complain.*

3. *Sure...go ahead — I don't want you to.*

4. *I'm not upset — Of course I'm upset, you moron!*

5. *You're certainly attentive tonight — Is sex all you ever think about?*

Source: Gallant, Jim "What Women Really Mean"
http://www.galisteao.com/gallant/humor/

16

THE MOMENT THEIR LIPS touched, Jessica's fears drifted away, and she was right there, right then, and there was nowhere else on earth she'd rather be.

His hand moved to her sash, which he opened effortlessly, then he slipped inside to touch her bare flesh. It felt as if he belonged there, as if without his touch she was incomplete. Everything that had troubled her diminished to insignificance as she explored his mouth, his taste, as he stroked her stomach with infinite care and respect.

As for her, she had her own tasks to complete, getting him naked first on the list. She got hold of his boxers and tugged down, but she was only able to get so far. Whispering a soft apology, he left her momentarily while he yanked the shorts off, and as long as he was in position, he spread her robe completely open, and when he lay down again it was flesh to flesh.

He lowered his head until he kissed her once more, but only a peck. Turning so he could nibble the edge of her chin, he whispered, "I don't understand this. How I feel when..."

"I know," she said. "It's crazy. But, oh, God."

"Uh-huh." He licked, then nibbled, then moved to her neck, kissing, murmuring sweet sounds that had no words, just the heat of his breath, the wet of his tongue, the sharpness of his teeth.

Distraction came when he cupped her breast, using the

flat of his palm to circle her nipple, brushing against it so lightly it was as if she imagined the caress.

Everything in her wanted more. "Please," she begged, pressing herself into his hand. "Don't make me wait."

He lifted his head and stared down at her. It was too dark and his face too shadowed to see him clearly, but the length of his pause made her think he could see her.

He said nothing as he moved on top of her, spreading her legs with his knees to nestle between them. Once settled, he found her hands, and slid his fingers between hers. He lifted both hands until they were above her head, brought them both together, then using one hand, so much larger than hers, he grasped both wrists tightly. When she tugged, he held her fast, immobile.

"What—?"

His low chuckle did all sorts of interesting things to her body. She tried to wiggle, but the way he held her captive, she could hardly move.

Spreading her legs farther, he touched her with his free hand, and after getting the lay of the land, he thrust a finger inside her, making her gasp with the sudden intrusion. The next second his mouth covered hers, swallowing her surprise as his finger plunged inside her.

There was nothing gentle or gentlemanly about anything he did. His tongue and his finger worked in rhythm, each taking her roughly, giving her no option but to surrender to the pleasure, to abandon herself to whatever wickedness was in store.

His body tensed as he ravaged her mouth, his fingers thrust inside her once more and then were gone, replaced quickly with the full length of him, filling her completely, making her gasp and arch her back.

He took her, plunged into her over and over roughly, the gentle man she'd known replaced by this animal presence, this predator.

She writhed beneath him, so awash with awareness and excitement she could hardly breathe. She heard herself moan, although the sound was unlike any she'd made before. Her hands struggled to break free even though she didn't want to be free. Her body was more hers than ever before, even as her moves were unfamiliar and jerky.

"Mine," he whispered gruffly, the tone brooking no quarter, taking possession of her body, her mind, her soul.

She wrapped her legs around his hips, meeting each thrust with one of her own, two bodies crashing together like waves to a craggy shore.

Her orgasm came quickly, with such ferociousness she could only cry out, inarticulate, trembling. She squeezed him both with her legs and with her inner muscles, and he went over the edge, too, his cry and hers twining like their bodies.

When it was over, he released her wrists, collapsing on top of her in a heap.

She didn't mind. She wanted to feel his chest rise and fall. She still had him inside her, and that she wasn't willing to relinquish.

Dizzy from the exertion, her body continued to spasm in echoes of the fierce climax, and every time she did, he answered in the same way.

Finally, long after the main event had ended, he sighed deeply, then kissed her. Gentle Dan had returned, but now she knew that there was another side to him, darker, rougher, and she wasn't sure which she preferred.

"I hate it," he said, "but I have to."

She whimpered. "Please, no."

"I must. Cramp in my leg."

She kissed his cheek. "Poor baby."

"It's your fault." He rolled off her, leaving her empty and chilled.

"How is it my fault?"

"You make me crazy. I have no self-control when I'm around you."

"That's not me. That's you."

"Nope. I know it's you."

"How?"

He turned his head to look at her. "Because it doesn't happen with anyone else."

"Oh."

He shook his head. "I don't know what to do with you."

"Me, neither."

"I keep thinking the best thing is to leave you alone. Go back to square one, and focus on the research. Get possessive around Owen, then back the hell off."

"That sounds right."

"But then we're alone, and I can't think about the research at all."

"I have no thoughts to spare. I have two more days of this campaign, and I can't let down my guard. It's everything I've worked toward and my future is tied to the outcome. So what do I do? I spend every free second thinking about you."

"It's a problem."

"No kidding."

He turned onto his side, propping his head up on his hand. "What are we going to do?"

"I have no idea."

"We could try again. Going back to the original deal, I mean. Look, but no touch. Questions, answers."

She nodded. "It won't be easy."

"Granted. But we're both adults. We should be able to curb our animal instincts for a couple of days."

"Right. Especially now that we've, uh…"

"Yes. Gotten our ya-yas out, so to speak."

"Well said." Jessica grinned. "So that's that. We'll be grown-ups. You'll sleep in here, I'll sleep in there. We'll talk. It'll be great." She turned onto her side, facing him, mimicking his posture exactly. "We'll be models of decorum."

"Platonic."

"Yet caring."

He frowned. "But you know, we've already kind of ruined tonight."

"Technically, you're right."

"So what I'm thinking is, let's just get all this sex business out of our systems. You know, boogie till we drop. Then it'll be easy to be paragons of virtue."

"I can see why you're so successful in business. You look at the big picture."

"Right. The kit *and* the caboodle."

"I figure," she said, "after I get a little water, maybe have a piece of fruit, we could meet in the bedroom."

"Ah, a change of venue."

She grinned. "Well, we wouldn't want to leave out anything."

"Wise, wise woman."

"Okay then. I'm going to drink and eat."

"I'm going to go to the bathroom, then join you."

She leaned over and kissed him. "Oh, goody."

"Amen to that."

HE WOKE UP to a note on the pillow instead of Jessica.

I've gone to Rockefeller Center to get ready for the Geocaching. I should be back by one.

That was it. Short and sweet and no mention at all of the night that had ended when the sun peeked over the skyscrapers.

He lay back down, debating the merits of really getting up, deciding in the end to stay put and order room service.

He knew Owen would be with Jessica at Rockefeller Center, but given the shape Dan was in, he wouldn't be much help until he got his act together.

Jessica had told him about the all-day stunt that would begin just after eight this morning. All the winners from a write-in campaign, almost a hundred of them, would be given portable global positioning systems and a map. Their task was basically a treasure hunt. Locate one Manhattan landmark by the longitude and latitude, find a clue to the next location, then the next, finally ending at the Central Park Pond, where one lucky winner would receive a full makeover, using New Dawn cosmetics, of course, a new wardrobe and a cruise for two to Jamaica. All of which was going to be recorded by as many entertainment-news organizations as Jessica could entice to be there.

It was quite a brilliant idea, really, but the logistics had been a daunting task. He knew for sure that all the clues were in place, and had been since last week. The grand prize had been buried last night.

At least the whole publicity monster would be over in a few days. He'd promised Jessica he would be there as her arm candy until it was finished, and he would. As for his own research project, he was more confused about women than ever. What was worse, none of his prepared questions seemed the least bit germane. He had no idea what to ask her, what would help him understand her. It seemed an unbridgeable chasm, his feelings, her feelings, their relationship, if he could even call it that. Perhaps if he knew what he wanted from her, it would help, but he didn't.

Okay, he knew some things: he wanted to see her again. To see her often. To pursue this—whatever it was. To make love to her. To see where she lived, how she lived, to learn about her past.

Shit, he wanted a lot, and almost none of it was directly related to his project.

Bottom line? No way he could walk away from her. She'd become important to him. Vitally. When he thought about a future without her he felt indescribably bleak.

Jessica had awakened something inside him that had been dormant. No other woman had affected him this way, and he had a sinking feeling that no other woman ever would. She was the spark that lit his fire. Maybe that was the whole thing about love. That you wander around until your dormant heart is awakened by the one other person on earth who matches some very specific requirements.

He winced as the full impact of his thoughts hit home. Love? He'd only known her for less than a week. Not enough time, surely, to go out on that limb. And yet, if it wasn't love, what was it? Lust didn't cover it. It was involved, but not the whole of it. He'd lusted often before, sometimes to the detriment of his health, his sanity. But that was child's play compared to his feelings now. He couldn't abide the thought of Jessica moving through life without him. But he had the distinct and uncomfortable suspicion that she didn't feel the same way.

Which basically meant he was screwed. Unless he could figure something out. In the next two days.

Right.

"ON YOUR MARK, get set, go!"

Jessica watched the contestants sprint across the Rockefeller Center Plaza, heading east toward the site of the first clue. The whir and click of hundreds of cameras sounded like a swarm of insects as journalists from around the world captured the moment. She'd gotten word early this morning that the sale of global positioning systems throughout the Greater New York Area had tripled in the last four days, and that all Manhattan was engaged in the largest treasure hunt in the city's history.

By all accounts, the event was a triumph. The name of

New Dawn had saturated the market on every level, print, radio, television and most importantly, word of mouth. Already Bloomingdale's, Saks, Barney's and hundreds of other retail stores were reporting record sales for a debuting cosmetics line. Everything Jessica had worked for over the last year was coming together in a beautifully wrapped package, and she knew that next week she was going to have to weigh offers from marketing and cosmetics firms from around the world.

She should have been floating on cloud nine. Instead, she had a king-size headache and a mad desire to steal the grand-prize cruise to Jamaica for herself.

Marla leaned against the brightly painted New Dawn pressmobile, arms crossed, a worried frown making her look younger than her twenty-four years. "Want to talk about it?"

Jessica shook her head. "I don't think so, but thanks."

"What time do we have to be at the park?"

"The soonest anyone can get there is four-thirty, so we'll set up at four."

Marla nodded. "Okay, see you there."

She didn't leave, however. She just kept staring.

"Marla, it's okay. I'm fine."

"You don't look fine."

"Don't let the New Dawn people hear you say that. I'm wearing all their best stuff."

Pushing herself off the van, Marla came to her side. "It's about Dan, isn't it?"

She was surprised by Marla's question. In all the time they'd worked together, Marla had never really asked her anything personal. Jessica hadn't allowed it. She'd realized when she first came up with this plan that things were going to change, but she'd never bargained on the major earthquake that had shaken her to the core. She sighed deeply and said, "Yeah, it's about Dan."

Marla took her by the elbow and led her toward a coffee kiosk. "I'll buy," she said. "You talk."

But Jessica didn't. Not until they had their drinks and found a table near the exit. "I don't know," she said finally. "Things are getting really complicated."

"How?"

Jessica studied her assistant, and it occurred to her that Marla could have been so much more than that. She could have been a friend. Her career wouldn't have been threatened, the campaign still would have been wildly successful. The only difference would have been that Jessica wouldn't have been so incredibly alone. "Obviously," she said, "this goes nowhere, but you were right about Dan. He isn't my old college boyfriend."

Marla didn't say anything. She just put her paper cup down on the table.

"He's a friend of a friend. I hired him to act like my boyfriend. You already figured out why."

"Oh."

"Yeah."

"Only now, you're kind of wishing he really was your boyfriend."

Jessica winced. "I'm not. At least I don't think I am. No, I'm not. I can't get involved. It goes against all my better judgment. Every woman I know in business has had to choose between love and real success. I don't want to have to make that choice."

"Love?"

Jessica felt the heat in her cheeks. "It was rhetorical."

"Right."

"No, I don't love him. At least, I don't think I do. It's just…"

"You can't stop thinking about him? You feel like you're a completely different person when he's near? You want to share every new sight and taste and sound with him? The whole universe has come into focus and you didn't even know it'd been blurry?''

She chuckled. ''Something like that.''

Marla leaned forward and touched her hand. The small gesture was completely foreign to their previous relationship, and yet at this moment, Jessica welcomed the kindness so much she actually teared up.

''Jessica, jobs come and go. But to lose someone like Dan…''

''It's not that simple.''

''It can be. If you let it.''

Jessica stared at her coffee, feelings she never would have imagined stirring deep inside, confusing her as nothing in her life had before. ''I don't know. I think I might know a way to have both him and my career.''

''Then go for it,'' Marla said. ''You deserve happiness, Jessica. Not just success.''

''I always thought success *was* happiness.''

''Oh, man,'' Marla said, leaning back on her chair. ''That's, well, kinda sad, isn't it?''

Jessica didn't answer. Not out loud, at least.

Top 5 things men know about women:

1.

2.

3.

4.

5.

17

JESSICA'S PACE down the hotel hallways slowed to just above a crawl as she approached her suite. Yes, she wanted to see Dan, but she still hadn't figured out the perfect way to ask him to be part of her grand plan.

Casual was the way to go, but not too casual; she didn't want him to feel peripheral, as if any man could do the trick. But she also didn't want to sound desperate and needy. If the plan was going to work, they both needed to want it. It would take some amount of coordination, and the whole scheme would crumple if Dan ended up feeling as if he wasn't getting enough of her time, or attention, or whatever. She had to be passionate about the benefits of the intermittent affair. He could feel completely unencumbered when he went off to do research or consulting, or climbing Everest. She would never be jealous or possessive. He could do as he pleased, as long as he was careful, and when they both deemed it time, they'd come together in what she fully expected to be a mind-blowing week of unadulterated bliss. Then they'd go to their separate corners until the next time.

Think of how much they would have to tell each other if they didn't see each other day after dull day. It would be like Christmas four times a year. Everything would be new and fresh and thrilling. In the downtimes, they could enjoy the benefits of singlehood, like not worrying about what time dinner was, or having to go to mind-numbing client parties.

To her mind, the arrangement was the best of all possible worlds. She just hoped like hell she could convince him. No. She would convince him. She was in the process of getting the whole world slathering to buy New Dawn cosmetics, and according to all reliable sources, she'd done just that. If she could convince a whole country, convincing one man would be a snap.

She finally reached her door. She slipped in the key card, turning the little light green, and went inside. "Hello?"

No answer. In her note she'd said she'd be back by one, and it was almost two. Dan had probably gotten bored and gone off for lunch.

Her shoulders relaxed as she put down her briefcase. What she wanted now was a bath. A big, long soak-extravaganza that would prune her skin and ease her aches. A nap would have been even more perfect, but she'd never trust herself to get up again. So a bath it would be.

She went to the bathroom and started the water in the big Roman tub. No jets, but plenty of room to stretch out. There was even a terry-bath pillow provided, along with two lilac-scented candles.

Her robe still hung on the bathroom door from this morning, so she didn't have to fetch that. She did, however, need to get her cell, despite the fact that if anyone had the nerve to call her, she'd cheerfully wring their necks. But she was technically on call, so…

Undressing slowly, she got all the way down to panties before pinning up her hair. She thought about applying a mud mask, but what if Dan came back? She didn't want to look like a Kabuki dancer.

The thought of him joining her in that great big tub gave her a little shiver, although really, she needed the rest. She'd decide if and when. No need to stress about it, or anything at the moment.

Peeling down her panties and tossing them in the corner,

she lit both candles, turned off the lights, then turned off the water, pleased at the billowing bubbles that she had brought forth. Already sighing, she tested the water with her big toe, then her foot. Satisfied that she wouldn't be scalded, she climbed into the tub, letting her body adjust in stages, until she lay neck high in happiness.

It took a couple of tries to get the pillow in exactly the right position, but it was worth it. She sighed one more time as she closed her eyes, her body floating, her mind at peace. All was right with her world.

She must have fallen asleep, because the sound of the door opening woke her with a start. She smiled, sinking down a little deeper into the water. Clearly she hadn't been out for long, because the water was still toasty and the bubbles hadn't dissipated.

"Hello," she said, her eyes still closed. "I'm so glad you're here."

Dan didn't say anything, but she could hear the soft plop of shirt and pants hit the tile.

She squirmed under the soft cover of bubbles, anticipating the wonderfulness of Dan plus bath plus soap plus her. It added up to one spectacular experience with the extra-added bonus of not having to clean up.

His feet hardly made a sound as they crossed the room. She opened her eyes languidly, focusing in on his good parts.

With a flash of horror, she realized they weren't his good parts at all.

It was Owen, wearing nothing but a pair of way-too-tight red bikini briefs, his chubby middle sticking out over the top. He smiled at her as if he were Brad Pitt, and if she hadn't been so damn frightened she would have laughed out loud.

She put her left hand over her cell phone and without

even looking at it, pressed speed-dial five. Then, very calmly, she said, "What are you doing, Owen?"

"I know all about your boyfriend."

"Oh?"

He moved over to the side of the tub, and for a horrifying minute she thought he was going to climb in with her. Instead, he sat on the edge, casually crossing his legs as if they were at the Manhattan Ocean Club instead of her bathroom. "Oh, yeah. I know it all."

"What do you know?"

"That you hired him. He's an actor. He doesn't mean a thing to you."

"Why do you think I did that, Owen?"

"Because you're afraid."

"Of what?"

He leaned slightly forward. "Of us."

"And why would I be afraid? Because you broke into my room, and came into my bathroom while I was taking a bath?"

Owen laughed.

She blessed New Dawn bubble bath for the lasting coverage as she prayed her ploy had worked. She'd never realized Owen was this far gone. Did he actually think she wanted him? That showing up in his underwear was going to do the trick?

"I know you've felt this…thing between us," he said. "I know you think it wouldn't work because of my wife, but you have to understand. I'm in love with you. Sure, my wife is great, she's a terrific person, but love? That hasn't been there for a long, long time."

"Does she know that, Owen?"

"Of course she does. She's very happy being a mother, being at home. She doesn't care what I do with my free time. In fact, she'd be delighted to get me out of her hair."

"So you've told her about us?"

"Sure, sure."

He stood, making her heart hammer in her chest. Maybe she should scream, but who would hear her if her cell phone call hadn't connected? This hotel was built when walls were walls and bathrooms were private. "Why don't we talk about it, Owen. In the living room. You go on out there, and I'll follow in a minute. I just need to freshen up a bit."

"You don't, Jessica. You're perfect the way you are." He sat again, his hand moving below the bubbles right into the water.

Jessica scooted all the way over, but if he made one more move, she'd have to do something. Screaming was out, but maybe she could take one of the candles and hit him in the head with it.

She glanced at the door, willing it to open.

"I'm afraid you've misunderstood something, Owen," she said. "Where did you get this wild idea about me hiring Dan?"

"This morning, when you were having coffee with Marla. I heard the whole thing."

She laughed, but it sounded unbelievably phony. "You heard things out of context. I didn't—"

"I heard every word. He's a whore, that's all. A gigolo. You don't feel anything at all for him. I heard you say it."

Just then the bathroom door swung open, and there was Dan, flanked on either side by two burly men in dark suits.

"Funny," Dan said. "I don't feel like a gigolo."

Owen sprang up from the side of the tub, crossing his hands in front of his privates like some kind of cartoon character. "Hey, what the hell?"

Dan held up his cell phone. "We heard it all. Especially the part about you breaking into her suite and her bathroom. You, sir, are about to find out how popular those red briefs are going to be on Rikers Island."

Owen blinked as though the whole thing was a bad dream. The two men, security for the hotel, walked over to him. It was clear they weren't interested in anything but removing Owen before there was a scene.

Dan stepped away from the door. "Don't worry, baby. The police are downstairs." Then he turned to McCabe. "I can't wait to see what the *New York Post* has to say about all this."

"My clothes," Owen said as each man took an arm. "At least let me get my pants. Do you know who I am? I'm a very important man. I can show you my ID if you let me get my—"

Dan swung the door shut behind them, then turned to her, his face creased in worry. "Are you all right?"

She nodded, although her whole body shivered uncontrollably. It felt as if she was in a tub of ice.

Dan got a towel and held it out for her. Jessica stood shakily and let him wrap her up. He held her close and tight, warming her as much from his concern as his body heat.

"I heard everything. I was downstairs in the café," he said.

"Thank God. For all I knew, you were in Hoboken."

"That bastard's gonna fry for this."

"I don't care about frying, but I'll make damn sure the president of the company hears about it. I just feel sorry for his wife and kids."

Dan pulled back for a second to look at her. "He didn't touch you, did he?"

She shook her head.

He smiled, kissed her, then pulled her back into his embrace. "I'm glad you trusted me to help."

She didn't answer, but the violent tremors had eased, and that was enough. "Come on," he said. "Let's get you in bed. You need to warm up."

"I can't. I have to go to Central Park."

"Marla can't handle that herself?"

"Not with Owen out of the picture."

After transferring the towel to her hands, he reluctantly let go. She shouldn't have to work now, not after that. Dan figured he'd call the police while Jessica got dressed and find out what they needed to do to press charges. Son of a bitch. He was almost sorry he'd brought the security men with him. He'd give anything to have five minutes alone with lover boy.

JESSICA WENT to her bedroom, a little surprised at how she was still shaking. Nothing had happened, except that Owen was no longer a problem. She hadn't been hurt, he hadn't even seen her naked. She'd have preferred not to have seen him in his underwear, but she doubted that would cause permanent trauma.

She was also surprised at how grateful she'd been to see Dan, and she wondered if she would have been just as happy to see anyone come to her rescue or if it was specifically Dan.

As she dressed, she ran her plan over one more time. The more often she heard it, the more logical it seemed. And now she knew that if all went according to plan, Dan was someone she could count on even if it wasn't one of their designated weeks. Good to know.

She'd had to count on herself alone for such a long time, she had mixed feelings about having someone else to turn to. Her father had died years ago, and her mother had never been someone to rely on, so it had all fallen on her shoulders. Getting into college, finding her first apartment, investing…she'd researched everything on her own. In that way, she supposed, she and Dan were alike. Although from what he'd said, he had his mother. She envied him what sounded like a great relationship. Although her lack of closeness with her family had given her free rein to pursue her own path with no interference whatsoever.

That was one of her fears about getting too involved with Dan. With anyone, for that matter. She didn't play well with others, never had. Her goals were always to be the leader, the field marshal, the captain. Never a follower. That's what made this job so important. After this, the real perk she'd receive in her new position, whatever it may be, would be freedom. She would be able to negotiate herself into a position of real power. No more Owens to contend with.

It was a solid plan, and given her success so far, it was going to turn out beautifully. It would be fascinating to see what came down about Owen. Geller and Patrick might just ask her to take his place. If they paid enough, she'd jump at the chance. There were so many things she wanted to implement in the company.

Dressed, she checked her look, ran a brush through her hair, and went back to the living room. Dan was just hanging up the phone.

"I'm going to the police station when you leave for Central Park. How long do you think you'll be?"

"God, hours. We have to wait until the last person checks in. It could be really late."

"What about dinner?"

"I'll send someone to pick up a pizza or something."

"Okay, I'll call before I join you, and see if you need food."

"Great. Thanks." She looked at her watch and saw she was late. Marla was probably pacing downstairs. She caught Dan around the waist, gave him a quick kiss, then said, "That thanks was for more than the offer of dinner."

"I know." He kissed her back, and then she was out the door, heading toward the elevator. It wasn't until the red light dinged that she realized she no longer needed Dan's services. Without Owen, she didn't need an escort at all.

IT WAS JUST AFTER nine-thirty when Dan left the police station. He made sure Owen wasn't going to walk away from this unscathed. In fact, he wanted him scathed to the max.

He held his arm out for a taxi as he dialed Jessica's cell phone. She answered after the fifth ring. Her hello was brief and harried, setting the tone.

"You want pizza?" he asked.

She paused.

He waited.

"Yes, please. Four or five big ones. A couple of just cheese, two pepperoni and one vegetarian."

"Got it. What about drinks."

"Don't worry about it. There's a vendor here."

"I'll be there in about forty-five minutes."

"Great. Oh, and Dan?"

A cab pulled over and he opened the door. "Yeah?"

"You don't have to do this, you know."

"I know. Now get back to work. I'll call if I'm going to be late."

"Okay," she said, then she was gone.

He gave the driver directions to his favorite pizza joint, which was pretty close to Central Park. He had the number in his phone book, so it was an easy matter to call. By the time he arrived, he could tell the cabbie to wait. If traffic were better, he could have had the whole thing taken care of in a half hour.

Leaning back, he took a long, deep breath. Ever since he'd gotten that weird call from Jessica, his heart had been pumping and he'd been wired. Totally ready for a fight, which wasn't real smart, because he'd gotten mighty testy with a cop at the precinct, and it was a very near thing that he wasn't keeping Owen the Rat Bastard company for the night.

He watched the passing people as they maneuvered through traffic, thinking how lucky he was to be heading toward Jessica. Someone had already won the cruise, he was sure. Maybe she would like to do that with him. Take a cruise. He hadn't been to Alaska in a long time. Or maybe she'd like to do a barge trip on the Seine.

He didn't give a damn, as long as it was with Jessica.

Tonight had made him more sure than ever that they needed to be together. She might be a tough cookie when it came to business, but she was still a woman, and he was still a man, and despite the incredible lack of political correctness, every instinct he had was to protect her, to care for her, to make sure no one would ever hurt her. He wanted to go to sleep with her right next to him. In fact, having her there felt like the only way he'd sleep well.

If Owen had hurt her…

Dan sighed. All was well, and Owen was safely out of the picture.

He swallowed hard as he sat up straight. "Shit," he whispered. He finally understood what Jessica meant when she said he "didn't have to."

He was officially out of a job.

Female Intuition

One day, three men were trekking through a jungle, when they came across a violent, raging river. They had no idea how to cross. So the first man decided to pray: "Please, God, give me the strength to cross this river." Immediately he grew enormous muscles in his arms and legs, and he managed to swim across the river in a couple of hours, nearly drowning twice.

The second man saw this and he prayed, "Please, God, give me the strength AND the tools to cross this river." A boat appeared from nowhere, and he battled across the river in an hour, nearly capsizing twice.

The third man saw this and prayed, "Please, God, give me the strength, the tools AND the intelligence to cross this river."

Immediately he turned into a woman. She looked at the map, walked upstream a hundred yards and crossed over the bridge to the other side.

Source: Thompson, Dave "Female Intuition"
http://www.ijmc.com/archives/

18

THE LAST OF the contestants found the Central Park Pond at 11:53 p.m. Jessica had let Marla and Shawn go home hours ago, the same for the rest of the support team. She gave the final couple their New Dawn gift basket and assured them that they could, indeed, keep the GPS.

Five minutes later, Jessica and Dan headed slowly toward East Fifty-ninth Street. She hadn't said anything to Marla about what happened with Owen. Her assistant would find out soon enough. In the meantime, she kept wondering what she should do about Dan. Ask him to leave?

The thought was far more upsetting than she ever would have imagined. She'd grown used to him being there for her.

All she wanted was to go back to the suite and crawl into bed with him. She could so readily imagine the comfort of his arms, and while she'd kept it together in front of the crowd, she felt very much in need of Dan's strength.

There wasn't much traffic at that time of night, including cabs. But Dan found them a ride, nonetheless. A hansom cab, complete with top-hatted driver and dappled-gray horse, and because of the hour, he arranged for the carriage to take them to the hotel.

Dan got in first, then held out his hand, which she took before she climbed up to the leather seat. He put his arm around her just as the horse lurched forward. It was late enough for the *clip-clop* of the horse's hooves to echo down the long street, broken from time to time by the roar of a speeding car, but those moments in between made Jessica feel as if she was somewhere else, someplace magical.

What in the world had happened to her in these few short days? Something magical? When was the last time she'd thought of anything so fanciful? Not since she'd been a girl, that's for sure. Her mother used to claim she was the dullest girl in all of Tulsa. The appellation made her cry the first time she'd heard it. But by the time she'd gotten her full scholarship to Harvard, she'd worn it as a badge of pride.

"Do you find me dull?" she asked.

His sharp bark of a laugh made her feel instantly better. "God, no. Why?"

"I was accused of dullness as a child. No one's ever made me feel it wasn't true, except you."

"I'd never call you dull. Driven, yes. Focused, absolutely. Obsessive—"

She put her fingers to his lips. "I got it. Thanks."

He captured her hand, kissed the back gently. "Are you all right?"

She nodded. "I wasn't, though. I was really shaken by Owen's intrusion."

"No wonder. It was a violation of your privacy, your trust."

"I think I would have handled it a lot better if I hadn't been naked."

"And I wouldn't have wanted to kill him in quite as many ways if you hadn't been naked."

She giggled. Something else she hadn't done since forever.

"I like that," he said, then he rested his head on hers.

"Like what?"

"The sound of you happy."

"I seem to make that sound a lot when I'm with you.

Which is odd, since I've spent the last five years trying very hard to be the toughest chick in the whole city. I'm with you four days, and I'm a giggling, sentimental fool.''

"Excellent."

She turned to look at him, dislodging him from his odd little perch. "Why is that excellent?"

"Because you befuddle me, too. It's nuts. But for the first time in years, something has become more important than my research projects. I didn't think it could happen."

"Is that why you haven't asked me any more questions?"

The carriage turned left and they both leaned into the side door. When they straightened, Dan cleared his throat. "Actually, there is one question I'd like to ask you."

Jessica sat a little straighter. "Only if you let me ask you something."

"You first," he said.

"Really?"

He nodded.

She took a deep breath, not sure at all her timing didn't suck. But he didn't have to stay, and she didn't want him to leave, so…

"I was thinking," she said, "about the end of all this. I mean, now that Owen's no longer a problem, the deal is pretty much null and void."

"Uh-huh."

She felt his hand on the back of her neck, just resting there. Long fingers, gentle pressure. It was a possessive move without being pushy or domineering. Perfect.

"I was thinking that we might like to, well, continue to see each other."

"Ah," he said.

"But not in the traditional sense. What I want to propose is something a little more unique."

His hand came off her neck, and she missed it. Looking

up at his face, she knew she had to explain fast because his eyebrows had furrowed something fierce.

"Hear me out before you decide." She shifted so she could see him more clearly. "It's been, I think you'll agree, a most remarkable week. It's obvious that the two of us have a special connection, that we mesh, sexually. We both have busy lives, we're both independent and not at all needy."

"What are you saying?"

"I'm saying I think we should get together a few times a year. I was actually thinking four times a year. For a week each time. We'd go somewhere no one knows us. Make love until we drop. No muss, no fuss. Just fun and sex and the delicious anticipation of doing it again in another three months."

"I see."

"You're not looking like this is a wonderful idea."

"No, no. I can certainly see where it would be quite advantageous."

"You hate it."

"Not at all. It makes sense. For you."

"But not for you."

He smiled, but the expression was more sad than anything else. "You know what my question was going to be?"

She shook her head, even though she was pretty sure she did.

"I want you to marry me, Jess. Not immediately, but not years away, either. I love you."

"You do?"

He nodded.

"But it's only been four days."

"I know. Doesn't matter."

"How can it not matter?"

"I've never experienced anything like what happens

when the two of us are together. The reason, aside from my complete distraction, that I haven't asked you more questions, is that for the first time in my life, I prefer the mystery. I like not being able to second-guess you. It's not frustrating at all, which I never would have believed. On the contrary, not knowing every little thing about you makes the days fascinating. I can't think of a better tomorrow and tomorrow than to unravel the mystery of you.''

Hot tears sprang to her eyes, and she blinked them back, turning her head away so he couldn't see. His words confused her more than any flat refusal. He wanted to marry her? It was everything she was afraid of, yet she was touched in a way that stunned her.

The idea was crazy, of course, but also kind of wonderful. "Dan, that's crazy."

"I know."

"The whole reason I hired you was because I didn't want any kind of commitment. Now that Owen's sure to be fired, it's all the more important that I stay clearheaded and focused. When I'm with you, I can't be all work. It's almost impossible to be any work at all."

"But that would change once we knew it was forever."

"Oh, really? Is that a promise?"

He looked at her for a long moment. "No. The truth is, I imagine you'll distract me forever. Not that I won't get anything done. It's just that you'll be there, too. You'll be there first."

"Which is just what I can't give you. Please, Dan, I swore I wouldn't put myself in a position where I had to choose between work and love. Don't make me go there. Take me up on my offer, okay? At least try it. We can meet in exactly three months. You pick the place and I'll be there. Whatever deal I get, I'll negotiate time away that week."

She touched his hand as the carriage pulled to a stop in front of their hotel. "Please, Dan?"

He took her by the shoulders and kissed her once, briefly. "I'll think about it."

"You're coming up tonight, right?"

"Yes, of course."

She exhaled with relief. She really didn't want to spend the night alone. "Thank you."

"You don't have to ask. You need me, I'm there."

She smiled, afraid to ask if he meant just for tonight, or for always. Surely he could see that it was not only premature to talk of marriage, but that marriage itself implied that the relationship was the most important thing in the world, which she couldn't, just couldn't agree to. Not when she was this close.

The doorman helped her down from the carriage. She hurried to the hansom driver to pay him before Dan climbed down. The tip was excessively large, but she didn't care. The deed was done by the time Dan joined her.

He smiled again, that strange edgy smile that made her nervous, but she didn't press him. If she just gave him time...

They walked hand in hand to the elevator, and she tried to read his expression in his reflection on the elevator door, but she couldn't.

Once in the room, he walked right over to the couch, pulling it out to make the bed.

Her heart sank. If he wasn't going to make love to her, then he certainly wasn't going to agree to her plan. She'd been crazy to hope.

"You don't really have to stay tonight," she said, passing him on her way to the bedroom. "If you'd rather be in your own bed, I understand."

"No, I'd like to stay. You had a rough day."

"Thank you," she said.

"What's on the agenda for tomorrow?"

"I have the feeling I'm going to be discussing the New Dawn account with the president of the company. Then there's the cocktail party here at the hotel."

"That's right. You'd better hurry then, get to bed. Best be on your toes when they start offering you the farm."

"I wish."

"They will," he said, his voice filled with confidence. "You're everything a company could ask for. They'd be insane not to give you the position."

"Thank you, Dan. That means a lot to me."

"It's simply the truth."

She turned, walked over to him, stood on her toes, and kissed him on the lips. "You're welcome in there," she whispered, nodding toward the bedroom.

"And for that, I'm most thankful, but it's probably better that you get some sleep. We don't tend to do that when I'm in there."

She sighed. "You're right. I'll be done in the bathroom soon."

"Take your time."

She wanted to say more, to add to her pitch, but she held back. Tomorrow. She was one hell of a marketing executive. He was only one man. She could change his mind. She had to.

DAN LAY AWAKE hour after hour, thinking about what Jessica had proposed. The plan was stunning in its simplicity, and on the face of it, the idea made perfect sense.

Oddly he hadn't considered the possibility at all, not even once.

So much about this week had been strange. His distraction, his attraction to a woman he'd barely spent time with, and yet it was all strangely familiar.

Because, he realized with a jolt, it reminded him so much of his parents.

They'd been with each other two days before they'd known. Actually, his mother had known the moment she met his father that they were going to be married. His father had taken an extra day because it was the night of an eclipse. A dumb excuse, but one he'd used since their wedding day.

Did he want this marriage to Jessica because he wanted the happiness his parents had found? Was he exaggerating his feelings for her?

He didn't think so. If there was one thing he was, it was self-critical. But this time, he just couldn't be sure.

There was only one thing to do. Agree to her plan until he was sure. If he still felt this way in three months, then there could be no doubt.

JESSICA WATCHED Dan from across the room. The cocktail party was the final event of the promotion, and everyone from the president of New Dawn cosmetics to the CEO of Time Warner had shown up. She was the darling of the marketing world and had received a dizzying array of offers. The most tempting, at the moment, was to take the executive vice presidency of Geller and Patrick, not replacing Owen, but in effect running the entire marketing and promotion for the global company. The money they'd offered her was in the astronomical range, and that had been the opening bid. When they got down to the nuts and bolts, she'd be talking six figures, penthouse apartment, use of the company jet and all the company penthouses around the world. She'd have more than she could have hoped for, her dreams exceeded.

Now, if only Dan would agree to her plan, her world couldn't look rosier. Unfortunately, he'd been vague about his decision. She wasn't sure what she had to do to convince him.

He laughed at something Marla said, and despite the crowded ballroom, his voice rose above the noise. It wasn't that he was so loud, just that he was so distinctive. At least to her.

Everything about him was unique. His attitude, his honesty, his style. She didn't want to lose him, and that was her biggest fear. If he didn't agree to their quarterly liaisons, what would she do? Say goodbye and never look back? How could she? On the other hand, how could she agree to a committed relationship when her career had to be her number one priority?

New Dawn was only one account, and it had swallowed up a year of her life. She couldn't count the nights she'd worked past midnight. She hadn't ever taken a full weekend off, not even during the holidays. How could she give him time where there was none?

Shawn, looking gorgeous in a dark gray Versace suit, joined Marla and Dan. He put his arm around Marla and they kissed briefly. He smiled at her, she smiled back, and even from this distance it was clear the two of them were in love.

They, too, had met this week. Marla had told her this afternoon that Shawn had asked her to accompany him on a trip to Montana, and that she'd accepted. While Jessica was happy for her, she wasn't certain that the two of them would work out. Sure, he seemed perfect, he seemed to care deeply for her, and Jessica felt certain that in his heart Shawn believed they were meant for each other. But how could they know? It was crazy for anyone to think that, after a few wild, exceptional days, love could happen. Real love. Not lust, but love.

Her gaze moved back to Dan. How could he know? It

didn't make sense, it wasn't logical, and it wasn't even smart.

Love was hard enough when all the circumstances were perfect. Her mother's best friend had been married over forty years, then found out her husband was having an affair. Their divorce had been a nightmare of bitterness and acrimony.

Jessica's aunt had been madly in love with an artist and had left her own career as a chemical engineer to follow him to Costa Rica. A year later, he'd spent all her savings and dumped her for a nineteen-year-old swimsuit model.

Sipping her martini, she headed toward the threesome, even though she should be schmoozing with the heavyweights all around her. At the very least she should be making nice to her boss.

"Hey, it's the woman of the year!" Marla said, grinning broadly. "Is it true?"

"What?" Jessica asked, her gaze skittering from Marla to Dan and back again.

"That you're going to be the new executive V.P. at Geller and Patrick?"

"Maybe. We're talking."

"Cool."

Jessica smiled. "If I do, that'll mean a hefty promotion for you."

Marla's grin flattened and her gaze moved away. Shawn tightened his hold on her, which she acknowledged with a nod. No way this was going to be good news.

"The thing is, Jessica…" Marla cleared her throat. "The thing is, I'm not sure I'm going to come back to work. After my vacation, I mean. Not that I wouldn't love to work with you again, but I might be, you know, moving. To Montana. With Shawn."

"Oh?"

"Yeah. It's kind of sudden and all, but see, he's been

planning this for a long time, and there's this ranch for sale. It's like his dream place, and there's no guarantee anything better would come along, so he's thinking that he might, well, take it.''

"And you'll take him."

Marla nodded, looking horribly guilty. "I'm positive no one better is going to come along." She kissed her guy.

"I don't want to move without her," Shawn said. "I'm crazy in love, and I want to start our new life away from all this madness."

Jessica leaned over and kissed Marla on the cheek. "I'm happy for you."

"Really?"

"Yes, really."

Marla's grin lit up her face. "What about you and Dan? Are you two an official item?"

Dan laughed. "No, more of an unofficial item. Your soon-to-be ex-boss has some intriguing ideas about the future that I've decided to look into."

Jessica swung around to look at him. Was this really his answer? "Seriously?"

He nodded. "Seriously."

She felt giddy with relief. "That's wonderful."

He walked closer to her, slipped his arm around her waist and kissed her on the lips, then he moved his mouth close to her ear. "It doesn't change how I feel," he whispered. "I love you. I want to marry you. But I can wait. At least for a little while."

She closed her eyes, wishing she could be more like Marla, but she wasn't. She was Jessica. Dull, obsessive, workaholic Jessica. She simply couldn't be another way.

A Real Man Would Do
These Things For His Girl

- *Call her the next day.*

- *Always laugh at her jokes.*

- *Tell her (truthfully) that he can't wait to see her again.*

- *Offer her a back rub without asking for one in return.*

- *Call her just to say you were thinking about her.*

- *Slow dance with her (not only on a dance floor).*

- *Bring her flowers for no reason.*

- *Tell her something about you that no one else knows.*

- *Remind her that you still think she's beautiful.*

- *Never stop trying to impress her.*

- *Tell her you love her.*

- *Give her great big hugs for no reason.*

Source: Bernard, Laura "How Men Could Win!"
http://www.angelfire.com/me/laurabernard/

19

DAN THOUGHT about letting his answering machine get the call; he was late for his mother's and he had serious penance to pay. His cat, the one he'd foolishly saved from a life on the streets, had not simply peed in her shoes, she'd left other…interesting…gifts in assorted drawers and cubbyholes. The mouse had been particularly odiferous, but the lizard had been the single biggest surprise. It had been a week since he'd taken the devil cat back, but his mother was still quite testy.

On the other hand, the phone call might be something important. He slammed his front door and dashed across the wooden floor to the phone, picking it up seconds before the machine would have kicked in.

"Dan, here."

Nothing. No breathing. Odd.

"Hello?"

"Hi."

Oh, shit. Dan stumbled back to his chair and sat down carefully. She wasn't supposed to be on the phone. They weren't supposed to talk for at least a month. Her rules. "Are you all right, Jess?"

"Yes, I'm fine."

"Oh. Well, that's good."

She cleared her throat.

He wondered where she was. He could go look at the

caller ID but he didn't. Given that it was only seven-thirty, she was undoubtedly still at the office.

"How are you?" she asked.

He had to smile. The woman was hideous at small talk. "I'm fine, Jessica. I'm great."

"Super. I'm glad."

He decided to wait. Something had to be going on for her to break the rules. It could be that she'd decided that the whole quarterly sexathon was a foolish notion. During the long week since they'd said goodbye, she could have come to her senses, realized that he was nothing but a nutcase.

On the other hand, maybe, like him, she'd realized that three months was an incredibly long time to wait. That the only time they had was now. That love could, indeed, happen in an instant.

"I took the job at Geller," she said finally.

"Fantastic. Tell me all about it."

"I want to, but not on the phone."

"Oh." His stomach sank. So it was the former, not the latter. She wanted to end it.

"No, oh, no, don't think that."

He frowned. "What?"

"Everything's still a go. It's just that, well, I miss you."

He grinned. Big-time. "That's excellent. I've missed you, too."

"So, uh, how about tomorrow? Lunch? One o'clock?"

"Yes, great. Sure. Anywhere."

"My assistant will call. I have to run. See you tomorrow."

"Okay," he said. "I love you." But she had already hung up.

JESSICA JUMPED out of the cab and adjusted her skirt as she hurried toward Dan's apartment. She was late. Again. Poor

Dan. So patient. And he hadn't once gotten on her case for tossing out her master plan like so much dross. In the last three weeks, she'd gone from seeing him once a week to twice a week to four times this week alone.

They'd grabbed a sandwich in her office. Eaten hot dogs from a pushcart. He'd cooked her dinner at her place twice, followed, of course, by two breakfasts.

He'd never said a word. Whenever they got together, they talked about her work, his work, Marla and Shawn, Owen's disgrace, his family, her family...and the odd thing about it was that her work hadn't suffered at all. In fact, if anything, he energized her. Unfailingly supportive, he understood the pressure of her new position, and he never complained when she had to take calls or change the schedule.

He'd gotten involved in a new project himself, which was as fascinating to her as it was to him. The new topic was the resurgence of subliminal advertising, debunked years ago, only to surface again in the age of the Internet.

She smiled at the doorman as he let her into the building, and took the slow elevator up by herself. Her heart beat faster as she reached his floor. But then, she'd come to expect that. Seeing Dan was the highlight of any day, of any night. She felt like a schoolgirl with a major crush every time she saw him, and tonight was no exception.

He opened the door with a smile so welcoming it gave her the shivers. God, he looked good. White oxford shirt, rolled sleeves, khaki slacks. His hair slightly disheveled and sexy as sin. She loved the way he looked at her. And when he kissed her hello, it was the same old thing: fireworks.

"You're stunning," he said, leading her into the apartment.

She smiled again as she saw the table, set beautifully

with china plates, a hothouse gardenia floating in a brandy snifter and shimmering candles. "Thank you."

"Success becomes you," he said, folding her into his arms.

She rested her head against his broad shoulder. "It's not success yet. But give me time."

"Nonsense. No matter what happens at the job, you've already won. You've gotten what you wanted, and done it through hard work and brilliance. What's not to like?"

She laughed. God, how he made her laugh. "I heard from Marla today."

He pulled back so he could see her face. "Oh?"

"She and Shawn set the date. They want us to come to the wedding."

"In Montana?"

She nodded. "Next month."

"Should be fun. Can you get away?"

"For a couple of days, sure. I wouldn't want to miss that."

"Great. I can make it, too."

"I haven't told you the date."

"Doesn't matter," he said. He folded his hand over hers. "I'm there."

She sniffed the air, fragrant with the scent of rosemary and cinnamon. "What is that?" she asked. "It smells heavenly."

He pulled out her chair, waited until she was seated, then headed toward the kitchen. "Chicken. One of my mother's special recipes. Why don't you pour us some wine while I get the food."

She did, enjoying the mellow Pinot Gris. He came back quickly, carrying a covered casserole, which he put in front of her. When he took off the lid, she sighed with contentment. "It looks fantastic."

He leaned over until his mouth was very close to hers. "So do you."

She kissed him back, and before she knew it, she was standing again in his arms and the enticing dinner wasn't nearly as appealing as getting her hands underneath his shirt.

He had his own agenda, and his was the more daunting task. She had on a jacket, a blouse, a bra, skirt, slip, panties. And yet, somehow, by the time they'd shuffled into the bedroom, between kisses, giggles and gasps, she was down to bra and panties while he still had on his pants.

His hands moved toward her bra clasp but she side-stepped out of his reach. "Wait," she said. "I want—"

He stopped her with a kiss. A long one, full of exploration and teasing. Distracting her just enough to undo her bra and slip the straps off her shoulders. It fell to the floor to join the rest of her strewn clothing, leaving her in high-cut bikini panties and black two-inch heels.

Dan stepped back, eyeing her from head to toe and back again. "Nice outfit."

"Thanks," she said. "How come you're still wearing pants?"

He looked down, feigning surprise. "Damn. I wondered why I was feeling so constricted." With a flourish, he undid his belt, his zipper, and after he stepped out of his jeans, he kicked them across the room, leaving him in a pair of silk boxers.

"That's quite a tent you've got there, mister."

"I'm a big believer in camping. Now, why is it that you still have clothes on?"

"Ah, so it's not just any camping. You like nudist camping."

"And I've got all sorts of activities planned."

She glanced at his big bed, which looked terribly inviting

with the fluffy green duvet and the overstuffed goose-down pillows. "Basket weaving?"

He stepped closer to her as she slipped her panties down until they pooled on her bra. "Naw, too corny. I thought we'd learn about tying knots."

Her head snapped up. "Oh?"

With a wicked grin he moved over to his nightstand and opened the drawer. He brought out two lengths of white rope. "Uh-huh."

"Wait a minute…"

"You remember that question I asked you?"

"Yes, I do."

"I was going to do this after dinner, but I'm flexible."

Her gaze stayed on the rope. It looked soft, but ropes? Being tied up?

He'd moved right in front of her, and his arms slipped around her back. "It's going to be wonderful," he whispered. "All you have to do is lie back and relax."

"I don't know about this, Camper Bob. I like to use my hands."

"Which is a good thing. Just not tonight. Tonight, you're going to be the pleasuree. Nothing but incredible things are going to happen to you. I promise."

She looked up into his eyes, but she already knew that he was telling her the truth. He would never do anything to harm her. On the contrary, he was the most considerate lover she'd ever dreamt of. Which didn't mean he couldn't get all caveman on her. She liked that a lot. He was spontaneous and thoughtful, and man, he could go the distance. "All right," she said, running her fingers down his back. "I'm yours. Do what you will."

He tried for an evil laugh, but the effect was ruined when he kissed her. She felt the tent pole against her hip and it occurred to her that they probably should hurry.

He must have thought the same thing, because he led her over to the bed. She went to sit on the edge, but he stopped her, opting instead to lift her into his arms and place her carefully in the center of the king-size mattress.

Once she was there, naked, vulnerable, he lifted her arms out to her sides, toward the posts.

Her heartbeat quickened as he tied her wrist, making sure that the bond wasn't too tight, but that she couldn't escape. She tested it a few times, almost told him to forget it, but then she decided she had nothing to lose by experimenting.

As he tied her other wrist, she realized there had never been anyone in her life she'd trust to do this. And certainly no other man had made her this anxious and wet. She squeezed her legs together, but it didn't help. Only one thing would.

She writhed on the comforter as he walked to the end of the bed. Smiling, taking her helpless body in with obvious delight, he shed his boxers. The "tent pole" was as stiff as she'd ever seen it, and she felt sexier than ever that she could have this effect on him.

Then he climbed onto the bed.

Her pulse raced, and despite her eagerness to try something new, her hands tugged at her bonds. It was impossible to simply lie still, especially when he lifted her right leg in his two hands, and kissed the top of her foot.

"Shh," he said. Then he kissed the top of her ankle, and with infinite patience and great care, he moved slowly up her leg, kissing, nibbling, licking.

She'd never thought of her leg as an erogenous zone, but clearly she'd been misinformed. Because every touch, every swipe of his tongue, every caress, made her insides go all gooey.

"Be still," he said.

"I can't."

He stopped moving until she met his gaze. "You can."

She understood what he was doing, and it excited her. Tonight, it was his ball game, not hers. Of course, she was the sole recipient of his total attention, which wasn't exactly a hardship, but still, she wasn't used to relinquishing power. In fact, her days were pretty much designed around the concept of gaining power.

Okay. She could be still. For now.

Once she acquiesced, he still didn't resume his ministrations until she'd lowered her gaze. Interesting. A little odd, but nice.

Especially nice because he moved more quickly up her thigh, kissing, sucking her flesh. All the wonderful things a mouth and tongue can do.

But that was only a prelude. The main action came a few moments later. His hands spread her thighs. She felt supernaked, unbelievably open, and a wee bit shy about it until she saw the hunger in his gaze.

That's all it took. That and his masterful tongue, of course. He knew exactly what to do, exactly how hard to push, when to slow down. He teased her until she begged, then rewarded her with the focus and attention of a Zen master.

She didn't come just once. Oh, no. If she'd had her hands free, she would have shifted, treated him to something devilish. But that wasn't what he wanted. And, in the end, it wasn't what she wanted either.

She came, crying out so loudly they probably heard her in the Bronx, three times. He just didn't let up. Not until she was so wiped out, her vision faded and her voice cracked.

Then he sat up. She managed to open her eyes enough to see his satisfied smile. But the biggest surprise was when her gaze moved down past his waist. He wasn't hard anymore.

He noticed her confusion. "Uh, the duvet is washable," he said.

Then she got it. He'd come without the slightest touch. He'd come because he'd made her crazy. Because he'd made her weep. Because he...

"Oh, God," she said, resting her head on the pillow. She still gasped for breath, and her body continued to shiver and quake as residual effects of her workout built and released. She felt sure that whatever pleasure sensors she had in her body were totally used up, completely empty of stores. Which was a good thing, indeed.

Somewhere out there, she felt him untie her wrists, and then he was next to her in the bed, with his arms and one leg around her. He nuzzled her neck with his soft lips, and she purred her satisfaction.

"So what did you think?" he asked.

She laughed. Well, as much as a laugh as she could muster. "Couldn't you tell?"

"Yeah, but I want to hear you say it."

She turned her head until her eyes met his. "You are an amazing man. I'd sign up for your camp any day."

"So the tying-up thing works for you?"

She nodded. "Maybe not as a steady diet. But the occasional dessert..."

"Or appetizer."

"Exactly."

"Oh, goody."

She giggled. "Dan, what am I going to do with you?"

He lifted his head. "Do you really want me to answer that?"

She thought for a long second, the butterflies in her stomach fluttering just enough to make her quite aware that she

knew what he was going to say. But she nodded anyway.
"Yes."

"You can marry me," he said. "Jess, I want you. I want
to go to bed with you every night. I want to wake up to
you every morning. I want to pack your lunch, and pick
out china patterns, and I want to hear everything about your
day, each day."

She studied his handsome face, the earnestness shining
in his hazel eyes. He loved her. There was no doubt about
it. He'd shown her in every way possible.

What he didn't know was that she'd been doing a private
research study of her own, which had nothing at all to do
with work. She'd been reading about love. About marriage.
About what makes it work.

What she'd discovered was that there is no magic answer. Just as Dan couldn't hope to find the secret to understanding women, she couldn't find the slightest hint of
a happily-ever-after formula.

There were no rules to follow, no game plan to stand
behind. The only guidelines she had were her own. What
did her heart tell her? What were her instincts about this
man, this future?

She shifted a bit, raised up on one elbow. "Can I tell
you something?"

"Of course."

"Here's what I know. I've never loved anyone before,
so I have no clue if I'm doing it the right way. I've certainly
never trusted anyone with my heart. You've seen what I
do, what I need to do, and all I've gotten from you is love,
support and confidence."

"But…?"

She smiled as she leaned forward and kissed him gently
on the lips. "So what do you say, Dan Crawford, that we
go up to Montana on our honeymoon?"

For a moment, his expression didn't change. Nothing. Then he smiled. Oh, what a smile.

"You're sure?" he asked.

She nodded. "Are you sure about me?"

"I told you once that I want to spend the rest of my life discovering the mystery of you. I haven't changed my mind."

She sighed. Turned once more so she was safe in the cocoon of his arms. His breath caressed her cheek. As she closed her eyes, she felt something new, something foreign. A second later it came to her... She was home.

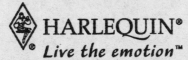

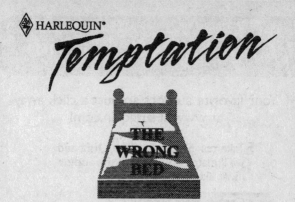

HARLEQUIN®

Temptation

THE WRONG BED

What happens when a girl finds herself in the *wrong* bed...with the *right* guy?

Find out in:

#866 NAUGHTY BY NATURE by Jule McBride
February 2002

#870 SOMETHING WILD by Toni Blake
March 2002

#874 CARRIED AWAY by Donna Kauffman
April 2002

#878 HER PERFECT STRANGER by Jill Shalvis
May 2002

#882 BARELY MISTAKEN by Jennifer LaBrecque
June 2002

#886 TWO TO TANGLE by Leslie Kelly
July 2002

Midnight mix-ups have never been so much fun!

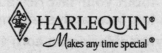

HARLEQUIN®
Makes any time special®

Visit us at www.eHarlequin.com

HTNBN2

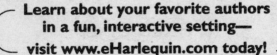

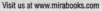

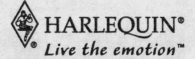

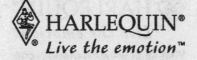

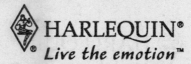